Books by Richard Matheson

STEEL

AND OTHER STORIES

RICHARD MATHESON

TOR®

A TOM DOHERTY ASSOCIATES BOOK
NEW YORK

This is a work of fiction. All of the characters, organizations, and events portrayed in these stories are either products of the author's imagination or are used fictitiously.

STEEL

A Tor Book
Published by Tom Doherty Associates, LLC
175 Fifth Avenue
New York, NY 10010

www.tor-forge.com

Tor® is a registered trademark of Tom Doherty Associates, LLC.

ISBN 978-0-7653-6761-7

First Edition: October 2011

Printed in the United States of America

0 9 8 7 6 5 4 3 2 1

CONTENTS

STEEL

AND OTHER STORIES

STEEL

The two men came out of the station rolling a covered object. They rolled it along the platform until they reached the middle of the train, then grunted as they lifted it up the steps, the sweat running down their bodies. One of its wheels fell off and bounced down the metal steps and a man coming up behind them picked it up and handed it to the man who was wearing a rumpled brown suit.

"Thanks," said the man in the brown suit and he put the wheel in his side coat pocket.

Inside the car, the men pushed the covered object down the aisle. With one of its wheels off, it was lopsided and the man in the brown suit—his name was Kelly—had to keep his shoulder braced against it to keep it from toppling over. He breathed heavily and licked away tiny balls of sweat that kept forming over his upper lip.

When they reached the middle of the car, the man in the wrinkled blue suit pushed forward one of the seat backs so there were four seats, two facing two. Then the two men pushed the covered object between the seats and Kelly reached through a slit in the covering and felt around until he found the right button.

The covered object sat down heavily on a seat by the window.

"Oh, God, listen to'm squeak," said Kelly.

The other man, Pole, shrugged and sat down with a sigh.

"What d'ya expect?" he asked.

Kelly was pulling off his suit coat. He dropped it down on the opposite seat and sat down beside the covered object.

"Well, we'll get 'im some o' that stuff soon's we're paid off," he said, worriedly.

"If we can find some," said Pole who was almost as

thin as one. He sat slumped back against the hot seat watching Kelly mop at his sweaty cheeks.

"Why shouldn't we?" asked Kelly, pushing the damp handkerchief down under his shirt collar.

"Because they don't make it no more," Pole said with the false patience of a man who has had to say the same thing too many times.

"Well, that's crazy," said Kelly. He pulled off his hat and patted at the bald spot in the center of his rust-colored hair. "There's still plenty B-twos in the business."

"Not many," said Pole, bracing one foot upon the covered object.

"*Don't*," said Kelly.

Pole let his foot drop heavily and a curse fell slowly from his lips, Kelly ran the handkerchief around the lining of his hat. He started to put the hat on again, then changed his mind and dropped it on top of his coat.

"Christ, it's hot," he said.

"It'll get hotter," said Pole.

Across the aisle a man put his suitcase up on the rack, took off his suit coat and sat down, puffing. Kelly looked at him, then turned back.

"Ya think it'll be hotter in Maynard, huh?" he asked.

Pole nodded. Kelly swallowed dryly.

"Wish we could have another o' them beers," he said.

Pole stared out the window at the heat waves rising from the concrete platform.

"I had three beers," said Kelly, "and I'm just as thirsty as I was when I started."

"Yeah," said Pole.

"Might as well've not had a beer since Philly," said Kelly.

Pole said, "Yeah."

Kelly sat there staring at Pole a moment. Pole had dark hair and white skin and his hands were the hands of a man who should be bigger than Pole was. But the hands were as clever as they were big. Pole's one o' the best, Kelly thought, one o' the best.

"Ya think he'll be all right?" he asked.

Pole grunted and smiled for an instant without being amused.

"If he don't get hit," he said.

"No, no, I mean it," said Kelly.

Pole's dark, lifeless eyes left the station and shifted over to Kelly.

"So do I," he said.

"Come *on*," Kelly said.

"Steel," said Pole, "ya know just as well as me. He's shot t'hell."

"That ain't true," said Kelly, shifting uncomfortably. "All he needs is a little work. A little overhaul 'n' he'll be good as new."

"Yeah, a little three-four grand overhaul," Pole said, "with parts they don't make no more." He looked out the window again.

"Oh . . . it ain't as bad as that," said Kelly. "Jesus, the way you talk you'd think he was ready for scrap."

"Ain't he?" Pole asked.

"No," said Kelly angrily, "he *ain't*."

Pole shrugged and his long white fingers rose and fell in his lap.

"Just cause he's a little old," said Kelly.

"Old." Pole grunted. "*Ancient.*"

"Oh . . ." Kelly took a deep breath of the hot air in the car and blew it out through his broad nose. He looked at the covered object like a father who was angry with his son's faults but angrier with those who mentioned the faults of his son.

"Plenty o' fight left in him," he said.

Pole watched the people walking on the platform. He

watched a porter pushing a wagon full of piled suit-cases.

"Well . . . is he okay?" Kelly asked finally as if he hated to ask.

Pole looked over at him.

"I dunno, Steel," he said. "He needs work. Ya know that. The trigger spring in his left arm's been rewired so many damn times it's almost shot. He's got no protection on that side. The left side of his face's all beat in, the eye lens is cracked. The leg cables is worn, they're pulled slack, the tension's gone to hell. Christ, even his gyro's off."

Pole looked out at the platform again with a disgusted hiss.

"Not to mention the oil paste he ain't got in 'im," he said.

"We'll get 'im some," Kelly said.

"Yeah, *after* the fight, *after* the fight!" Pole snapped. "What about *before* the fight? He'll be creakin' around that ring like a goddamn—*steam shovel*. It'll be a miracle if he goes two rounds. They'll prob'ly ride us outta town on a rail."

Kelly swallowed. "I don't think it's that bad," he said.

"The *hell* it ain't, said Pole. "It's worse. Wait'll that crowd gets a load of 'Battling' Maxo from Philadelphia.

Oh—*Christ*, they'll blow a nut. We'll be lucky if we get our five hundred bucks."

"Well, the contract's signed," said Kelly firmly. "They can't back out now. I got a copy right in the old pocket." He leaned over and patted at his coat.

"That contract's for Battling Maxo," said Pole. "Not for this—steam shovel here."

"Maxo's gonna do all right," said Kelly as if he was trying hard to believe it. "He's not as bad off as you say."

"Against a B-*seven?*" Pole asked.

"It's just a *starter* B-seven," said Kelly. "It ain't got the kinks out yet."

Pole turned away.

"Battling Maxo," he said. "One-round Maxo. The battling steam shovel."

"Aw, shut the hell up!" Kelly snapped suddenly, getting redder. "You're always knockin' 'im down. Well, he's been doin' okay for twelve years now and he'll keep on doin' okay. So he needs some oil paste. And he needs a little work. *So what?* With five hundred bucks we can get him all the paste he needs. And a new trigger spring for his arm and—and new leg cables! And everything. Chris-*sake.*"

He fell back against the seat, chest shuddering with

breath and rubbed at his cheeks with his wet handkerchief. He looked aside at Maxo. Abruptly, he reached over a hand and patted Maxo's covered knee clumsily and the steel clanked hollowly under his touch.

"You're doin' all right," said Kelly to his fighter.

The train was moving across a sun-baked prairie. All the windows were open but the wind that blew in was like blasts from an oven.

Kelly sat reading his paper, his shirt sticking wetly to his broad chest. Pole had taken his coat off too and was staring morosely out the window at the grass-tufted prairie that went as far as he could see. Maxo sat under his covering, his heavy steel frame rocking a little with the motion of the train.

Kelly put down his paper.

"Not even a word," he said.

"What d'ya expect?" Pole asked. "They don't cover Maynard."

"Maxo ain't just some clunk from Maynard," said Kelly. "He was big time. Ya'd think they'd"—he shrugged—"remember him."

"Why? For a coupla prelims in the Garden three years ago?" Pole asked.

"It wasn't no three years, buddy," said Kelly.

"It was in 1994," said Pole, "and now it's 1997. That's three years where I come from."

"It was late '94," said Kelly. "Right before Christmas. Don't ya remember? Just before—Marge and me . . ."

Kelly didn't finish. He stared down at the paper as if Marge's picture were on it—the way she looked the day she left him.

"What's the difference?" Pole asked. "They don't remember *them* for Chrissake. With a coupla thousand o' the damn things floatin' around? How could they remember 'em? About the only ones who get space are the champeens and the new models."

Pole looked at Maxo. "I hear Mawling's puttin' out a B-nine this year," he said.

Kelly refocused his eyes. "Yeah?" he said uninterestedly.

"Hyper-triggers in both arms—*and* legs. All steeled aluminum. Triple gyro. Triple-twisted wiring. God, they'll be beautiful."

Kelly put down the paper.

"Think they'd remember him," he muttered. "It wasn't so long ago."

His face relaxed in a smile of recollection.

"Boy, will I ever forget that night?" he said. "No one gives us a tumble. It was all Dimsy the Rock, Dimsy the Rock. *Three* t'one for Dimsy the Rock. Dimsy the Rock— fourth rankin' light heavy. On his way t'the top."

He chuckled deep in his chest. "And did we ever put him away," he said. "*Oooh.*" He grunted with savage pleasure. "I can see that left cross now. *Bang!* Right in the chops. And old Dimsy the Rock hittin' the canvas like a—like a *rock*, yeah, *just* like a rock!"

He laughed happily. "Boy, what a night, what a night," he said. "Will I ever forget that night?"

Pole looked at Kelly with a somber face. Then he turned away and stared at the dusty sun-baked plain again.

"I wonder," he muttered.

Kelly saw the man across the aisle looking again at the covered Maxo. He caught the man's eye and smiled, then gestured with his head toward Maxo.

"That's my fighter," he said, loudly.

The man smiled politely, cupping a hand behind one ear.

"My fighter," said Kelly. "Battling Maxo. Ever hear of 'im?"

The man stared at Kelly a moment before shaking his head.

Kelly smiled. "Yeah, he was almost light heavyweight champ once," he told the man. The man nodded politely.

On an impulse, Kelly got up and stepped across the aisle. He reversed the seatback in front of the man and sat down facing him.

"Pretty damn hot," he said.

The man smiled. "Yes. Yes it is," he said.

"No new trains out here yet, huh?"

"No," said the man. "Not yet."

"Got all the new ones back in Philly," said Kelly. "That's where"—he gestured with his head—"my friend 'n I come from. And Maxo."

Kelly stuck out his hand.

"The name's Kelly," he said. "Tim Kelly."

The man looked surprised. His grip was loose.

"Maxwell," he said.

When he drew back his hand he rubbed it unobtrusively on his pants leg.

"I used t'be called 'Steel' Kelly," said Kelly. "Used

t'be in the business m'self. Before the war o' course. I was a light heavy."

"Oh?"

"Yeah. That's right. Called me 'Steel' cause I never got knocked down once. Not *once*. I was even number nine in the ranks once. Yeah."

"I see." The man waited patiently.

"My fighter," said Kelly, gesturing toward Maxo with his head again. "He's a light heavy too. We're fightin' in Maynard t'night. You goin' that far?"

"Uh—no," said the man. "No, I'm—getting off at Hayes."

"Oh." Kelly nodded. "Too bad. Gonna be a good scrap." He let out a heavy breath. "Yeah, he was—fourth in the ranks once. He'll be back too. He—uh—knocked down Dimsy the Rock in late '94. Maybe ya read about that."

"I don't believe . . ."

"Oh. Uh-huh." Kelly nodded. "Well . . . it was in all the East Coast papers. You know. New York, Boston, Philly. Yeah it—got a hell of a spread. Biggest upset o' the year."

He scratched at his bald spot.

"He's a B-two y'know but—that means he's the second model Mawling put out," he explained, seeing the look on the man's face. "That was back in—let's see—'90, I think it was. Yeah, '90."

He made a smacking sound with his lips. "Yeah, that was a good model," he said. "The best. Maxo's still goin' strong." He shrugged depreciatingly. "I don't go for these new ones," he said. "You know. The ones made o' steeled aluminum with all the doo-dads."

The man stared at Kelly blankly.

"Too— . . . flashy—flimsy. Nothin' . . ." Kelly bunched his big fist in front of his chest and made a face. "Nothin' *solid*," he said. "No. Mawling don't make 'em like Maxo no more."

"I see," said the man.

Kelly smiled.

"Yeah," he said. "Used t'be in the game m'self. When there was enough men, o' course. Before the bans." He shook his head, then smiled quickly. "Well," he said, "we'll take this B-seven. Don't even know what his name is," he said, laughing.

His face sobered for an instant and he swallowed.

"We'll take 'im," he said.

Later on, when the man had gotten off the train, Kelly went back to his seat. He put his feet up on the opposite seat and, laying back his head, he covered his face with the newspaper.

"Get a little shut-eye," he said.

Pole grunted.

Kelly sat slouched back, staring at the newspaper next to his eyes. He felt Maxo bumping against his side a little. He listened to the squeaking of Maxo's joints. "Be all right," he muttered to himself.

"What?" Pole asked.

Kelly swallowed. "I didn't say anything," he said.

When they got off the train at six o'clock that evening they pushed Maxo around the station and onto the sidewalk. Across the street from them a man sitting in his taxi called them.

"We got no taxi money," said Pole.

"We can't just push 'im through the streets," Kelly said. "Besides, we don't even know where Kruger Stadium is."

"What are we supposed to eat with then?"

"We'll be loaded after the fight," said Kelly. "I'll buy you a steak three inches thick."

Sighing, Pole helped Kelly push the heavy Maxo

across the street that was still so hot they could feel it through their shoes. Kelly started sweating right away and licking at his upper lip.

"God, how d'they live out here?" he asked.

When they were putting Maxo inside the cab the base wheel came out again and Pole, with a snarl, kicked it away.

"What're ya *doin'*?" Kelly asked.

"Oh . . . sh—" Pole got into the taxi and slumped back against the warm leather of the seat while Kelly hurried over the soft tar pavement and picked up the wheel.

"Chris-*sake*," Kelly muttered as he got in the cab. "What's the—?"

"Where to, chief?" the driver asked.

"Kruger Stadium," Kelly said.

"You're there." The cab driver pushed in the rotor button and the car glided away from the curb.

"What the hell's wrong with you?" Kelly asked Pole in a low voice. "We wait more'n half a damn year t'get us a bout and you been nothin' but bellyaches from the start."

"Some bout," said Pole. "Maynard, Kansas—the prize-fightin' center o' the nation."

"It's a start, ain't it?" Kelly said. "It'll keep us in coffee 'n' cakes a while, won't it? It'll put Maxo back in shape. And if we take it, it could lead to—"

Pole glanced over disgustedly.

"I don't *get* you," Kelly said quietly. "He's our fighter. What're ya writin' 'im off for? Don't ya want 'im t'win?"

"I'm a class-A mechanic, Steel," Pole said in his falsely patient voice. "I'm not a day-dreamin' kid. We got a piece o' dead iron here, not a B-seven. It's simple mechanics, Steel, that's all. Maxo'll be lucky if he comes out o' that ring with his head still on."

Kelly turned away angrily.

"It's a *starter* B-seven," he muttered. "Full o' kinks. *Full* of 'em."

"Sure, sure," said Pole.

They sat silently a while looking out the window, Maxo between them, the broad steel shoulders bumping against theirs. Kelly stared at the building, his hands clenching and unclenching in his lap as if he was getting ready to go fifteen rounds.

"That a B-fighter ya got there?" the driver asked over his shoulder.

Kelly started and looked forward. He managed a smile.

"That's right," he said.

"Fightin' t'night?"

"Yeah. Battling Maxo. Maybe ya heard of 'im."

"Nope."

"He was almost light heavyweight champ once," said Kelly.

"That right?"

"Yes, sir. Ya heard o' Dimsy the Rock, ain't ya?"

"Don't think so."

"Well, Dimsy the—"

Kelly stopped and glanced over at Pole who was shifting irritably on the seat.

"Dimsy the Rock was number *three* in the light heavy ranks. Right on his way t'the top they all said. Well, my boy put 'im away in the fourth round. Left-crossed 'im—*bang!* Almost put Dimsy through the ropes. It was beautiful."

"That right?" asked the driver.

"Yes sir. You get a chance, stop by t'night at the stadium. You'll see a good fight."

"Have you seen this Maynard Flash?" Pole asked the driver suddenly.

"The Flash? You bet. Man, there's a fighter on his way. Won seven straight. He'll be up there soon, ya can bet ya life. Matter o' fact he's fightin' t'night too. With some B-two heap from back East I hear."

The driver snickered. "Flash'll slaughter 'im," he said.

Kelly stared at the back of the driver's head, the skin tight across his cheek bones.

"Yeah?" he said, flatly.

"Man, he'll—"

The driver broke off suddenly and looked back. "Hey, you ain't—" he started, then turned front again. "Hey, I didn't know, mister," he said. "I was only ribbin'."

"Skip it," Pole said. "You're right."

Kelly's head snapped around and he glared at the sallow-face Pole.

"*Shut up*," he said in a low voice.

He fell back against the seat and stared out the window, his face hard.

"I'm gonna get 'im some oil paste," he said after they'd ridden a block.

"Swell," said Pole. "We'll eat the tools."

"Go to hell," said Kelly.

The cab pulled up in front of the brick-fronted stadium and they lifted Maxo out onto the sidewalk. While Pole tilted him, Kelly squatted down and slid the base wheel back into its slot. Then Kelly paid the driver the exact fare and they started pushing Maxo toward the alley.

"Look," said Kelly, nodding toward the poster board in front of the stadium. The third fight listed was

MAYNARD FLASH

(B-7, L.H.)

VS.

BATTLING MAXO

(B-2, L.H.)

"Big deal," said Pole.

Kelly's smile disappeared. He started to say something, then pressed his lips together. He shook his head irritably and big drops of his sweat fell to the sidewalk.

Maxo creaked as they pushed him down the alley and carried him up the steps to the door. The base wheel fell out again and bounced down the cement steps. Neither one of them said anything.

It was hotter inside. The air didn't move.

"Refreshing like a closet," Pole said.

"Get the wheel," Kelly said and started down the

narrow hallway leaving Pole with Maxo. Pole leaned Maxo against the wall and turned for the door.

Kelly came to a half-glassed office door and knocked.

"Yeah," said a voice inside. Kelly went in, taking off his hat.

The fat bald man looked up from his desk. His skull glistened with sweat.

"I'm Battling Maxo's owner," said Kelly, smiling. He extended his big hand but the man ignored it.

"Was wonderin' if you'd make it," said the man whose name was Mr. Waddow. "Your fighter in decent shape?"

"The best," said Kelly cheerfully. "The best. My mechanic—he's class-A—just took 'im apart and put 'im together again before we left Philly."

The man looked unconvinced.

"He's in good shape," said Kelly.

"You're lucky t'get a bout with a B-two," said Mr. Waddow. "We ain't used nothin' less than B-fours for more than two years now. The fighter we was after got stuck in a car wreck though and got ruined."

Kelly nodded. "Well, ya got nothin' t'worry about," he said. "My fighter's in top shape. He's the one knocked down Dimsy the Rock in Madison Square year or so ago."

"I want a good fight," said the fat man.

"You'll get a good fight," Kelly said, feeling a tight pain in his stomach muscles. "Maxo's in good shape. You'll see. He's in top shape."

"I just want a good fight."

Kelly stared at the fat man a moment. Then he said, "You got a ready room we can use? The mechanic 'n' me'd like t'get something t'eat."

"Third door down the hall on the right side," said Mr. Waddow. "Your bout's at eight thirty."

Kelly nodded. "Okay."

"Be there," said Mr. Waddow turning back to his work.

"Uh . . . what about—?" Kelly started.

"You get ya money after ya deliver a fight," Mr. Waddow cut him off.

Kelly's smile faltered.

"Okay," he said. "See ya then."

When Mr. Waddow didn't answer, he turned for the door.

"Don't slam the door," Mr. Waddow said. Kelly didn't.

"Come on," he said to Pole when he was in the hall again. They pushed Maxo down to the ready room and put him inside it.

"What about checkin' 'im over?" Kelly said.

"What about my *gut?*" snapped Pole. "I ain't eaten in six hours."

Kelly blew out a heavy breath. "All right, let's go then," he said.

They put Maxo in a corner of the room.

"We should be able t'lock him in," Kelly said.

"Why? Ya think somebody's gonna *steal* 'im?"

"He's valuable," said Kelly.

"Sure, he's a priceless antique," said Pole.

Kelly closed the door three times before the latch caught. He turned away from it, shaking his head worriedly. As they started down the hall he looked at his wrist and saw for the fiftieth time the white band where his pawned watch had been.

"What time is it?" he asked.

"Six twenty-five," said Pole.

"We'll have t'make it fast," Kelly said. "I want ya t'check 'im over good before the fight."

"What for?" asked Pole.

"Did ya *hear* me?" Kelly said angrily.

"Sure, sure," Pole said.

"He's gonna take that son-of-a-bitch B-seven," Kelly said, barely opening his lips.

"Sure he is," said Pole. "With his teeth."

"Hurry up," Kelly said, ignoring him. "We ain't got all night. Did ya get the wheel?"

Pole handed it to him.

"Some town," Kelly said disgustedly as they came back in the side door of the stadium.

"I told ya they wouldn't have any oil paste here," Pole said. "Why should they? B-twos are dead. Maxo's probably the only one in a thousand miles."

Kelly walked quickly down the hall, opened the door of the ready room and went in. He crossed over to Maxo and pulled off the covering.

"Get to it," he said. "There ain't much time."

Blowing out a slow, tired breath, Pole took off his wrinkled blue coat and tossed it over the bench standing against the wall. He dragged a small table over to where Maxo was, then rolled up his sleeves. Kelly took off his hat and coat and watched while Pole worked loose the nut that held the tool cavity door shut. He stood with his big hands on his hips while Pole drew out the tools one by one and laid them down on the table.

"Rust," Pole muttered. He rubbed a finger around

the inside of the cavity and held it up, copper colored rust flaking off the tip.

"Come on," Kelly said, irritably. He sat down on the bench and watched as Pole pried off the sectional plates on Maxo's chest. His eyes ran up over Maxo's leonine head. If I didn't see them coils, he thought once more, I'd swear he was real. Only the mechanics in a B-fight could tell it wasn't real men in there. Sometimes people were actually fooled and sent in letters complaining that real men were being used. Even from ringside the flesh tones looked human. Mawling had a special patent on that.

Kelly's face relaxed as he smiled fondly at Maxo.

"Good boy," he murmured. Pole didn't hear. Kelly watched the sure-handed mechanic probe with his electric pick, examining connections and potency centers.

"Is he all right?" he asked, without thinking.

"Sure, he's great," Pole said. He plucked out a tiny steel-caged tube. "If this doesn't blow out," he said.

"Why should it?"

"It's sub-par," Pole said jadedly. "I told ya that after the last fight *eight months* ago."

Kelly swallowed. "We'll get 'im a new one after this bout," he said.

"Seventy-five bucks," muttered Pole as if he were watching the money fly away on green wings.

"It'll hold," Kelly said, more to himself than to Pole.

Pole shrugged. He put back the tube and pressed in the row of buttons on the main autonomic board. Maxo stirred.

"Take it easy on the left arm," said Kelly. "Save it."

"If it don't work here, it won't work out there," said Pole.

He jabbed at a button and Maxo's left arm began moving with little, circling motions. Pole pushed over the safety-block switch that would keep Maxo from counter-punching and stepped back. He threw a right at Maxo's chin and the robot's arm jumped up with a hitching motion to cover his face. Maxo's left eye flickered like a ruby catching the sun.

"If that eye cell goes . . ." Pole said.

"It *won't*," said Kelly tensely. He watched Pole throw another punch at the left side of Maxo's head. He saw the tiny ripple of the flexo-covered cheek, then the arm jerked up again. It squeaked.

"That's enough," he said. "It works. Try the rest of 'im."

"He's gonna get more than two punches throwed at his head," Pole said.

"*His arm's all right,*" Kelly said. "Try something else I said."

Pole reached inside Maxo and activated the leg cable centers. Maxo began shifting around. He lifted his left leg and shook off the base wheel automatically. Then he was standing lightly on his black-shoed feet, feeling at the floor like a cured cripple testing for stance.

Pole reached forward and jabbed in the FULL button, then jumped back as Maxo's eye beams centered on him and the robot moved forward, broad shoulders rocking slowly, arms up defensively.

"Christ," Pole muttered, "they'll hear 'im squeakin' in the back row."

Kelly grimaced, teeth set. He watched Pole throw another right and Maxo's arm lurch raggedly. His throat moved with a convulsive swallow and he seemed to have trouble breathing the close air in the little room.

Pole shifted around the floor quickly, side to side. Maxo followed lumberingly, changing direction with visibly jerking motions.

"Oh, he's *beautiful*," Pole said, stopping. "Just beautiful." Maxo came up, arms still raised, and Pole jabbed in under them, pushing the OFF button. Maxo stopped.

"Look, we'll have t'put 'im on defense, Steel," Pole said. "That's all there is to it. He'll get chopped t'pieces if we have 'im movin' in."

Kelly cleared his throat. "No," he said.

"Oh for—will ya use ya *head?*" snapped Pole. "He's a B-two f'Chrissake. He's gonna get slaughtered anyway. Let's save the pieces."

"They want 'im on the *offense*," said Kelly. "It's in the contract."

Pole turned away with a hiss.

"What's the use?" he muttered.

"Test 'im some more."

"What for? He's as good as he'll ever be."

"Will ya do what I say!" Kelly shouted, all the tension exploding out of him.

Pole turned back and jabbed in a button. Maxo's left arm shot out. There was a snapping noise inside it and it fell against Maxo's side with a dead clank.

Kelly started up, his face stricken. "Jesus, what did ya *do!*" he cried. He ran over to where Pole was pushing the button again. Maxo's arm didn't move.

"I *told* ya not t'fool with that arm!" Kelly yelled. "What the hell's the *matter* with ya!" His voice cracked in the middle of the sentence.

Pole didn't answer. He picked up his pry and began working off the left shoulder plate.

"So help me God, if you broke that arm . . ." Kelly warned in a low, shaking voice.

"If *I* broke it!" Pole snapped. "Listen, you dumb mick! This heap has been runnin' on borrowed time for three years now! Don't talk t'me about breakages!"

Kelly clenched his teeth, his eyes small and deadly.

"Open it up," he said.

"Son-of-a—" Pole muttered as he got the plate off. "You find another goddamn mechanic that coulda kep' this steam shovel together any better these last years. You just *find* one."

Kelly didn't answer. He stood rigidly, watching while Pole put down the curved plate and looked inside.

When Pole touched it, the trigger spring broke in half and part of it jumped across the room.

Kelly stared at the shoulder pit with horrified eyes.

"Oh, Christ," he said in a shaking voice. "Oh, *Christ*."

Pole started to say something, then stopped. He looked at the ashen-faced Kelly without moving.

Kelly's eyes moved to Pole.

"Fix it," he said, hoarsely.

Pole swallowed. "Steel, I—"

"*Fix* it!"

"I can't! That spring's been fixin' t'break for—"

"You broke it! Now *fix* it!" Kelly clamped rigid fingers on Pole's arm. Pole jerked back.

"Let go of me!" he said.

"What's the matter with you!" Kelly cried. "Are you crazy? He's got t'be fixed. He's *got* t'be!"

"Steel, he needs a new spring."

"Well, *get* it!"

"They don't *have* 'em here, Steel," Pole said. "I *told* ya. And if they *did* have 'em, we ain't got the sixteen-fifty t'get one."

"Oh—Oh, *Jesus*," said Kelly. His hand fell away and he stumbled to the other side of the room. He sank down on the bench and stared without blinking at the tall motionless Maxo.

He sat there a long time, just staring, while Pole stood watching him, the pry still in his hand. He saw Kelly's broad chest rise and fall with spasmodic movements. Kelly's face was a blank.

"If he don't watch 'em," muttered Kelly, finally.

"What?"

Kelly looked up, his mouth set in a straight, hard line. "If he don't watch, it'll work," he said.

"What're ya talkin' about?"

Kelly stood up and started unbuttoning his shirt.

"What're ya—"

Pole stopped dead, his mouth falling open. "Are you *crazy?*" he asked.

Kelly kept unbuttoning his shirt. He pulled it off and tossed it on the bench.

"Steel, you're out o' your mind!" Pole said. "You can't do that!"

Kelly didn't say anything.

"But you'll—Steel, you're *crazy!*"

"We deliver a fight or we don't get paid," Kelly said.

"But—Jesus, you'll get *killed!*"

Kelly pulled off his undershirt. His chest was beefy, there was red hair swirled around it. "Have to shave this off," he said.

"Steel, *come on*," Pole said. "You—"

His eyes widened as Kelly sat down on the bench and started unlacing his shoes.

"They'll never let ya," Pole said. "You can't make 'em think you're a—" He stopped and took a jerky step forward. "Steel, fuh Chrissake!"

Kelly looked up at Pole with dead eyes.

"You'll help me," he said.

"But they—"

"Nobody knows what Maxo looks like," Kelly said. "And only Waddow saw me. If he don't watch the bouts we'll be all right."

"But—"

"They won't know," Kelly said. "The B's bleed and bruise too."

"Steel, *come on*," Pole said shakily. He took a deep breath and calmed himself. He sat down hurriedly beside the broad-shouldered Irishman.

"Look," he said. "I got a sister back East—in Maryland. If I wire 'er, she'll send us the dough t'get back."

Kelly got up and unbuckled his belt.

"Steel, I know a guy in Philly with a B-five, wants t'sell cheap," Pole said desperately. "We could scurry up the cash and—Steel, fuh Chrissake, you'll get *killed!* It's a B-seven! Don't ya understand? A B-*seven!* You'll be mangled!"

Kelly was working the dark trunks over Maxo's hips.

"I won't let ya do it, Steel," Pole said. "I'll go to—"

He broke off with a sucked-in gasp as Kelly whirled and moved over quickly to haul him to his feet. Kelly's grip was like the jaws of a trap and there was nothing left of him in his eyes.

"You'll help me," Kelly said in a low, trembling voice. "You'll help me or I'll beat ya brains out on the wall."

"You'll get killed," Pole murmured.

"Then I will," said Kelly.

Mr. Waddow came out of his office as Pole was walking the covered Kelly toward the ring.

"Come on, come on," Mr. Waddow said. "They're waitin' on ya."

Pole nodded jerkily and guided Kelly down the hall.

"Where's the owner?" Mr. Waddow called after them.

Pole swallowed quickly. "In the audience," he said.

Mr. Waddow grunted and, as they walked on, Pole heard the door to the office close. Breath emptied from him.

"I should've told 'im," he muttered.

"I'd o' killed ya," Kelly said, his voice muffled under the covering.

Crowd sounds leaked back into the hall now as they turned a corner. Under the canvas covering, Kelly felt a drop of sweat trickle down his temple.

"Listen," he said, "you'll have t'towel me off between rounds."

"Between what rounds?" Pole asked tensely. "You won't even last one."

"Shut up."

"You think you're just up against some tough fighter?" Pole asked. "You're up against a machine! Don't ya—"

"I said shut up."

"Oh . . . you dumb—" Pole swallowed. "If I towel ya off, they'll know," he said.

"They ain't seen a B-two in years," Kelly broke in. "If anyone asks, tell 'em it's an oil leak."

"Sure," said Pole disgustedly. He bit his lips. "Steel, ya'll never get away with it."

The last part of his sentence was drowned out as, suddenly, they were among the crowd, walking down the sloping aisle toward the ring. Kelly held his knees locked and walked a little stiffly. He drew in a long, deep breath and let it out slowly. He'd have to breathe in small gasps and exhalations through his nose while he was in the ring. The people couldn't see his chest moving or they'd know.

The heat burdened in around him like a hanging weight. It was like walking along the sloping floor of an ocean of heat and sound. He heard voices drifting past him as he moved.

"Ya'll take 'im home in a box!"

"Well, if it ain't *Rattlin'* Maxo!"

And the inevitable, "*Scrap iron!*"

Kelly swallowed dryly, feeling a tight drawing sensation in his loins. Thirsty, he thought. The momentary vision of the bar across from the Kansas City train station crossed his mind. The dim-lit booth, the cool fan breeze on the back of his neck, the icy, sweat-beaded bottle chilling his palm. He swallowed again. He hadn't allowed himself one drink in the last hour. The less he drank the less he'd sweat, he knew.

"Watch it."

He felt Pole's hand slide in through the opening in the back of the covering, felt the mechanic's hand grab his arm and check him.

"Ring steps," Pole said out of a corner of his mouth.

Kelly edged his right foot forward until the shoe tip touched the riser of the bottom step. Then he lifted his foot to the step and started up.

At the top, Pole's fingers tightened around his arm again.

"Ropes," Pole said, guardedly.

It was hard getting through the ropes with the covering on. Kelly almost fell and hoots and catcalls came at him like spears out of the din. Kelly felt the canvas give slightly under his feet and then Pole pushed the stool against the back of his legs and he sat down a little too jerkily.

"Hey, get that derrick out o' here!" shouted a man in the second row. Laughter and hoots. "Scrap iron!" yelled some people.

Then Pole drew off the covering and put it down on the ring apron.

Kelly sat there staring at the Maynard Flash.

The B-seven was motionless, its gloved hands hanging across its legs. There was imitation blond hair, crew cut, growing out of its skull pores. Its face was that of an impassive Adonis. The simulation of muscle curve on its body and limbs was almost perfect. For a moment Kelly almost thought that years had been peeled away and he was in the business again, facing a young contender. He swallowed carefully. Pole crouched beside him, pretending to fiddle with an arm plate.

"Steel, *don't*," he muttered again.

Kelly didn't answer. He felt a desperate desire to suck in a lungful of air and bellow his chest. He drew in small patches of air through his nose and let them trickle out. He kept staring at the Maynard Flash, thinking of the array of instant-reaction centers inside that smooth arch of chest. The drawing sensation reached his stomach. It was like a cold hand pulling in at strands of muscle and ligament.

A red-faced man in a white suit climbed into the ring and reached up for the microphone which was swinging down to him.

"Ladies and gentlemen," he announced, "the opening bout of the evening. A ten-round light heavyweight bout. From Philadelphia, the B-two, *Battling Maxo.*"

The crowd booed and hissed. They threw up paper airplanes and shouted "*Scrap iron!*"

"His opponent, our own B-seven, the *Maynard Flash!*"

Cheers and wild clapping. The Flash's mechanic touched a button under the left armpit and the B-seven jumped up and held his arms over his head in the victory gesture. The crowd laughed happily.

"Jesus," Pole muttered, "I never saw that. Must be a new gimmick."

Kelly blinked to relieve his eyes.

"Three more bouts to follow," said the red-faced man and then the microphone drew up and he left the ring. There was no referee. B-fighters never clinched—their machinery rejected it—and there was no knock-down count. A felled B-fighter stayed down. The new B-nine, it was claimed by the Mawling publicity staff, would be able to get up, which would make for livelier and longer bouts.

Pole pretended to check over Kelly.

"Steel, it's your last chance," he begged.

"*Get out*," said Kelly without moving his lips.

Pole looked at Kelly's immobile eyes a moment, then sucked in a ragged breath and straightened up.

"Stay away from him," he warned as he started through the ropes.

Across the ring, the Flash was standing in its corner, hitting its gloves together as if it were a real young fighter anxious to get the fight started. Kelly stood up and Pole drew the stool away. Kelly stood watching the B-seven, seeing how its eye centers were zeroing in on him. There was a cold sinking in his stomach.

The bell rang.

The B-seven moved out smoothly from its corner with a mechanical glide, its arms raised in the traditional way, gloved hands wavering in tiny circles in front of it. It moved quickly toward Kelly who edged out of his corner automatically, his mind feeling, abruptly, frozen. He felt his own hands rise as if someone else had lifted them and his legs were like dead wood under him. He kept his gaze on the bright unmoving eyes of the Maynard Flash.

They came together. The B-seven's left flicked out and Kelly blocked it, feeling the rock-hard fist of the Flash even through his glove. The fist moved out again. Kelly drew back his head and felt a warm breeze across his mouth. His own left shot out and banged against the Flash's nose. It was like hitting a door knob. Pain flared in Kelly's arm and his jaw muscles went hard as he struggled to keep his face blank.

The B-seven feinted with a left and Kelly knocked it aside. He couldn't stop the right that blurred in after it and grazed his left temple. He jerked his head away and the B-seven threw a left that hit him over the ear. Kelly lurched back, throwing out a left that the B-seven brushed aside. Kelly caught his footing and hit the Flash's jaw solidly with a right uppercut. He felt a jolt of pain run up his arm. The Flash's head didn't budge. He shot out a left that hit Kelly on the right shoulder.

Kelly back-pedaled instinctively. Then he heard someone yell, "Get 'im a bicycle!" and he remembered what Mr. Waddow had said. He moved in again, his lips aching they were pressed together so tightly.

A left caught him under the heart and he felt the impact shudder through his frame. Pain stabbed at his heart. He threw a spasmodic left which banged against the B-seven's nose again. There was only pain. Kelly stepped back and staggered as a hard right caught him high on the chest. He started to move back. The B-seven hit him on the chest again. Kelly lost his balance and stepped back quickly to catch equilibrium. The crowd booed. The B-seven moved in without making a single mechanical sound.

Kelly regained his balance and stopped. He threw a hard right that missed. The momentum of his blow threw him off center and the Flash's left drove hard against his upper right arm. The arm went numb. Even as Kelly was sucking in a teeth-clenched gasp the B-seven shot in a hard right under his guard that slammed into Kelly's spongy stomach. Kelly felt the breath go out of him. His right slapped ineffectively across the Flash's right cheek. The Flash's eyes glinted.

As the B-seven moved in again, Kelly side-stepped and, for a moment, the radial eye centers lost him. Kelly moved out of range dizzily, pulling air in through his nostrils.

"Get that heap out o' there!" some man screamed.

"Scrap iron, scrap iron!"

Breath shook in Kelly's throat. He swallowed quickly and started forward just as the Flash picked him up again. Taking a chance, he sucked in breath through his mouth hoping that his movements would keep the people from seeing. Then he was up to the B-seven. He stepped in close, hoping to out-time electrical impulse, and threw a hard right at the Flash's body.

The B-seven's left shot up and Kelly's blow was deflected by the iron wrist. Kelly's left was thrown off too and then the Flash's left shot in and drove the breath out of Kelly again. Kelly's left barely hit the Flash's rock-hard chest. He staggered back, the B-seven following. He kept jabbing but the B-seven kept deflecting the blows and counterjabbing with almost the same piston-like motion. Kelly's head kept snapping back. He fell back more and saw the right coming straight at him. He couldn't stop it.

The blow drove in like a steel battering-ram. Spears of pain shot behind Kelly's eyes and through his head. A black cloud seemed to flood across the ring. His muffled cry was drowned out by the screaming crowd as he toppled back, his nose and mouth trickling bright blood that looked as good as the dye they used in the B-fighters.

The rope checked his fall, pressing in rough and hard against his back. He swayed there, right arm hanging limp, left arm raised defensively. He blinked his eyes instinctively, trying to focus them. I'm a robot, he thought, a robot.

The Flash stepped in and drove a violent right into Kelly's chest, a left to his stomach. Kelly doubled over, gagging. A right slammed off his skull like a hammer blow, driving him back against the ropes again. The crowd screamed.

Kelly saw the blurred outline of the Maynard Flash. He felt another blow smash into his chest like a club. With a sob he threw a wild left that the B-seven brushed off. Another sharp blow landed on Kelly's shoulder. He lifted his right and managed to deflect the worst of a left thrown at his jaw. Another right concaved his stomach. He doubled over. A hammering right drove him back on the ropes. He felt hot salty blood in his mouth and the roar of the crowd seemed to swallow him. Stay up!—he screamed at himself. Stay up goddamn you! The ring wavered before him like dark water.

With a desperate surge of energy, he threw a right as hard as he could at the tall beautiful figure in front of him. Something cracked in his wrist and hand and a wave of searing pain shot up his arm. His throat-locked cry went unheard. His arm fell, his left went down and the crowd shrieked and howled for the Flash to finish it.

There was only inches between them now. The B-seven rained in blows that didn't miss. Kelly lurched and staggered under the impact of them. His head snapped from side to side. Blood ran across his face in scarlet ribbons His arm hung like a dead branch at his side. He kept getting slammed back against the ropes, bouncing forward and getting slammed back again. He couldn't see any more. He could only hear the screaming of the crowd and the endless swishing and thudding of the B-seven's gloves. Stay up, he thought. I have to stay up. He drew in his head and hunched his shoulders to protect himself.

He was like that seven seconds before the bell when a clubbing right on the side of his head sent him crashing to the canvas.

He lay there gasping for breath. Suddenly, he started to get up, then, equally as suddenly, realized that he couldn't. He fell forward again and lay on his stomach on the warm canvas, his head throbbing with pain. He could hear the booing and hissing of the dissatisfied crowd.

When Pole finally managed to get him up and slip the

cover over his head the crowd was jeering so loudly that Kelly couldn't hear Pole's voice. He felt the mechanic's big hand inside the covering, guiding him, but he fell down climbing through the ropes and almost fell again on the steps. His legs were like rubber tubes. Stay up. His brain still murmured the words.

In the ready room he collapsed. Pole tried to get him up on the bench but he couldn't. Finally, he bunched up his blue coat under Kelly's head and, kneeling, he started patting with his handkerchief at the trickles of blood.

"You dumb bastard," he kept muttering in a thin, shaking voice. "You dumb bastard."

Kelly lifted his hand and brushed away Pole's hand.

"Go—get the—money," he gasped hoarsely.

"What?"

"The *money!*" gasped Kelly through his teeth.

"But—"

"*Now!*" Kelly's voice was barely intelligible.

Pole straightened up and stood looking down at Kelly a moment. Then he turned and went out.

Kelly lay there drawing in breath and exhaling it with wheezing sounds. He couldn't move his right hand and he knew it was broken. He felt the blood trickling from his nose and mouth. His body throbbed with pain.

After a few moments he struggled up on his left elbow and turned his head, pain crackling along his neck muscles. When he saw that Maxo was all right he put his head down again. A smile twisted up one corner of his lips.

When Pole came back, Kelly lifted his head painfully. Pole came over and knelt down. He started patting at the blood again.

"Ya get it?" Kelly asked in a crusty whisper.

Pole blew out a slow breath.

"*Well?*"

Pole swallowed. "Half of it," he said.

Kelly stared up at him blankly, his mouth fallen open. His eyes didn't believe it.

"He said he wouldn't pay five C's for a one rounder."

"What d'ya mean?" Kelly's voice cracked. He tried to get up and put down his right hand. With a strangled cry he fell back, his face white. His head thrashed on the coat pillow, his eyes shut tightly.

"*No*," he moaned. "No. No. No. No. No."

Pole was looking at his hand and wrist. "*Jesus God,*" he whispered.

Kelly's eyes opened and he stared up dizzily at the mechanic.

"He can't—he can't do that," he gasped.

Pole licked his dry lips.

"Steel, there—ain't a thing we can do. He's got a bunch o' toughs in the office with 'im. I can't . . ." He lowered his head. "And if—you was t'go there he'd know what ya done. And—he might even take back the two and a half."

Kelly lay on his back, staring up at the naked bulb without blinking. His chest labored and shuddered with breath.

"No," he murmured. "No."

He lay there for a long time without talking. Pole got some water and cleaned off his face and gave him a drink. He opened up his small suitcase and patched up Kelly's face. He put Kelly's right arm in a sling.

Fifteen minutes later Kelly spoke.

"Well go back by bus," he said.

"What?" Pole asked.

"We'll go by bus," Kelly said slowly. "That'll only cost, oh, fifty-sixty bucks." He swallowed and shifted on his back. "That'll leave almost two C's. We can get 'im a—a new trigger spring and a—eye lens and—" He blinked his eyes and held them shut a moment as the room started fading again.

"And oil paste," he said then. "Loads of it. He'll be—good as new again."

Kelly looked up at Pole. "Then we'll be all set up," he said. "Maxo'll be in good shape again. And we can get us some decent bouts." He swallowed and breathed laboriously. "That's all he needs is a little work. New spring, a new eye lens. That'll shape 'im up. We'll show those bastards what a B-two can do. Old Maxo'll show 'em. *Right?*"

Pole looked down at the big Irishman and sighed.

"Right, Steel," he said.

TO FIT THE CRIME

"I've been murdered!" cried ancient Iverson Lord, "brutally, foully murdered!"

"There, there," said his wife.

"Now, now," said his doctor.

"Garbage," murmured his son.

"As soon expect sympathy from mushrooms!" snarled the decaying poet. "From cabbages!"

"From kings," said his son.

The parchment face flinted momentarily, then sagged into meditative creases. "Aye, they will miss me," he sighed. "The kings of language, the emperors of the tongue." He closed his eyes. "The lords of splendrous symbol, they shall know when I have passed."

The moulding scholar lay propped on a cloudbank of pillows. A peak of silken dressing gown erupted his turkey throat and head. His head was large, an eroded football with lace holes for eyes and a snapping gash of a mouth.

He looked over them all; his wife, his daughter, his son and his doctor. His beady suspicious eyes played about the room. He glared at the walls. "Assassins," he grumbled.

The doctor reached for his wrist.

"Avaunt!" snapped the hunched-over semanticist, clawing out. "Take off your clumsy fingers!"

He threw an ired glance at the physician. "White-collar witch doctors," he accused, "who take the Hypocratic Oath and mash it into common vaudeville."

"Iverson, your wrist," said the doctor.

"Who knuckle-tap our chests and sound our hearts yet have no more conception of our ills than plumbers have of stars or pigs of paradise."

"Your wrist, Iverson," the doctor said.

Iverson Lord was near ninety. His limbs were glass-like and brittle. His blood ran slow. His heartbeat was a largo drum. Only his brain hung clear and unaffected, a last soldier defending the fort against senility.

"I refuse to die," he announced as if someone had suggested it. His face darkened. "I will not let bleak nature dim my light nor strip the jewel of being from my fingers!"

"There, there," said his wife.

"*There, there! There, there!*" rasped the poet, false teeth clicking in an outrage. "What betrayal is this! That I, who shape my words and breathe into their forms the breath of might, should be a-fettered to this cliché-ridden imbecile!"

Mrs. Lord submitted her delicate presence to the abuse of her husband. She strained out a peace-making smile which played upon her features of faded rose. She plucked feebly at mouse-gray curls.

"You're upset, Ivie dear," she said.

"Upset!" he cried. "Who would not be upset when set upon by gloating jackals!"

"Father," his daughter implored.

"Jackals, whose brains like sterile lumps beneath their skulls refuse to emanate the vaguest glow of insight into words."

He narrowed his eyes and gave his life-long lecture once again. "Who cannot deal with word cannot deal with thought," he said. "Who cannot deal with thought should be dealt with—mercilessly!" He pounded a strengthless fist on the counterpane.

"Words!" he cried. "Our tools, our glory and our welded chains!"

"You'd better save your strength," his son suggested.

The jade eyes stabbed up, demolishing. Iverson Lord curled thin lips in revulsion.

"*Bug*," he said.

His son looked down on him. "Compose your affairs, Father," he said. "Accept. You'll find death not half bad."

"I am not dying!" howled the old poet. "You'd murder me, wouldn't you! Thug! I shall not listen further!"

He jerked up the covers and buried his white-crowned head beneath them. His scrawny, dry fingers dribbled over the sheet edge.

"Ivie, dear," entreated his wife. "You'll smother yourself."

"Better smothered than betrayed!" came the muffled rejoinder.

The doctor drew back the blankets.

"Murdered!" croaked Iverson Lord at all of them, "brutally, foully murdered!"

"Ivie, dear, no one has murdered you," said his wife. "We've tried to be good to you."

"*Good!*" He grew apoplectic. "Mute good. Groveling good. *Insignificant* good. Ah! That I should have created the barren flesh about this bed of pain."

"Father, don't," begged his daughter.

Iverson Lord looked upon her. A look of stage indulgence flickered on his face.

"So Eunice, my bespectacled owl," he said, "I suppose you are as eager as the rest to view your sire in the act of perishing."

"Father, don't talk that way," said myopic Eunice.

"What way, Eunice, my tooth-ridden gobbler—my erupted Venus? In literate English? Yes, perhaps that does put rather a strain on your embalmed faculties."

Eunice blinked. She accepted.

"What will you do, child," inquired Iverson Lord, "when I am taken from you? Who will speak to you? Indeed, who will even look?" The old eyes glittered a *coup de grâce*. "Let there be no equivocation, my dear," he said gently. "You are ugly in the extreme."

"Ivie, dear," pleaded Mrs. Lord.

"Leave her alone!" said Alfred Lord. "Must you destroy everything before you leave?"

Iverson Lord raised a hackle.

"*You*," he intoned, darting a fanged glance. "Mental vandal. Desecrator of the mind. Defacing your birthright in the name of business. Pouring your honored blood into the sewers of commerciality."

His stale breath fluttered harshly. "Groveler before check books," he sneered. "Scraper before bank accounts."

His voice strained into grating falsetto. "*No*, madame. *Assuredly*, madame. I kiss with reverent lips your fat, unwholesome mind, *Madame!*"

Alfred Lord smiled now, content to let the barrages of his father fall upon himself.

"Let me remind you," he said, "of the importance of the profit system."

"Profit system!" exploded his sire. "Jungle system!"

"Supply and demand," said Alfred Lord.

"Alfred, don't," Eunice cautioned.

Too late to prevent venous eyeballs from threatening to discharge from their sockets. "Judas of the brain!" screamed the poet. "Boy scout of intellect!"

"I pain to mention it," Alfred Lord still dropped

coals, "but even a businessman may, tentatively, accept Christianity."

"Christianity!" snapped the jaded near-corpse, losing aim in his fury. "Outmoded bag of long-suffering beans! Better the lions had eaten all of them and saved the world from a bad bargain!"

"That will do, Iverson," said the doctor. "Calm yourself."

"You're upset, Ivie," said his wife. "Alfred, you mustn't upset your father."

Iverson Lord's dulling eyes flicked up final lashes of scorn at his fifty-year whipping post.

"My wife's capacity for intelligible discourse," he said, "is about that of primordial gelatine."

He patted her bowed head with a smile. "My dear," he said, "you are nothing. You are absolutely nothing."

Mrs. Lord pressed white fingers to her cheek. "You're upset, Ivie," her frail voice spoke. "You don't mean it."

The old man sagged back, dejected.

"This is my penitence," he said, "to live with this woman who knows so little of words she cannot tell insult from praise."

The doctor beckoned to the poet's family. They moved from the bed toward the fireplace.

"That's right," moaned the rotting scholar, "desert me. Leave me to the rats."

"No rats," said the doctor.

As the three Lords moved across the thick rug they heard the old man's voice.

"You've been my doctor twenty years," it said. "Your brain is varicosed." "I am to perish," it bemoaned, "sans pity, sans hope, sans all." "Words," it mused. "Build me a sepulcher of words and I shall rise again."

And domineered: "This is my legacy! To all semantic drudges—irreverence, intolerance and the generation of unbridled dismay!"

The three survivors stood before the crackling flames.

"He's disappointed," said the son. "He expected to live forever."

"He *will* live forever," Eunice emoted. "He is a great man."

"He's a little man," said Alfred Lord, "who is trying to get even with nature for reducing his excellence to usual dust."

"Alfred," said his mother. "Your father is old. And . . . he's afraid."

"Afraid, perhaps. Great? No. Every spoken cruelty,

every deception and selfishness has reduced his greatness. Right now he's just an old, dying crank."

Then they heard Iverson Lord. "Sweep her away!" howled the sinking poet. "Whip her away with nine-tails of eternal life!"

The doctor was trying to capture the flailing wrist. They all moved hastily for the bed.

"Arrest her!" yelled Iverson Lord. "Let her not embrace me as her lover! Avaunt—black, foul-faced strumpet!" He took a sock at her. "Avaunt, I say!"

The old man collapsed back on his pillow. His breath escaped like faltering steam. His lips formed soundless, never-to-be-known quatrains. His gaze fused to the ceiling. His hands twitched out a last palsied gesture of defiance. Then he stared at the ceiling until the doctor reached out adjusting fingers.

"It's done," the doctor said.

Mrs. Lord gasped. "*No*," she said. She could not believe.

Eunice did not weep. "He is with the angels now," she said.

"Let justice be done," said the son of dead Iverson Lord.

. . .

It was a gray place.

No flames. No licking smoke. No pallor of doom obscured his sight. Only gray—mediocre gray—unrelieved gray.

Iverson Lord strode through the gray place.

"The absence of retributive heat and leak-eyed wailing souls is pre-eminently encouraging," he said to himself.

Striding on. Through a long gray hall.

"After-life," he mused. "So all is not symbolic applesauce as once I had suspected."

Another hallway angled in. A man came walking out briskly. He joined the scholar. He clapped him smartly on the shoulder.

"Greetings, mate!" said the man.

Iverson Lord looked down his mobile, Grecian nose.

"I beg your pardon," he said, distaste wrinkling his words.

"What do you know?" said the man. "How's life treating you? What do you know and what do you say?"

The semanticist drew back askance. The man forged on, arms and legs pumping mightily.

"What's new?" he was saying. "Give me the low-down. Give me the dirt."

Two side halls. The man buzzed into one gray length. Another man appeared. He walked beside Iverson Lord. The poet looked at him narrowly. The man smiled broadly.

"Nice day, isn't it?" he said.

"What place is this?" asked Iverson Lord.

"Nice weather we've been having," said the man.

"I ask, what place is this?"

"Looks like it might turn out nice," said the man.

"Craven!" snapped Iverson Lord, stopping in his tracks. "Answer me!"

The man said, "Everybody complains about the weather but nobody . . ."

"Silence!"

The semanticist watched the man turn into a side hall-way. He shook his head. "Grotesque mummery," he said.

Another man appeared.

"Hi, you!" cried Iverson Lord. He ran. He clutched the man's gray sleeve. "What place is this?"

"You don't say?" said the man.

"You will answer me, sirrah!"

"Is that a fact?" said the man.

The poet sprayed wrath upon the man. His eyes popped.

He grabbed at the man's gray lapels. "You shall give intelligence or I shall throttle you!" he cried.

"Honest?" said the man.

Iverson Lord gaped. "What density is this?" he spoke incredulously. "Is this man or vegetable in my hands?"

"Well, knock me down and pick me up," said the man.

Something barren and chilling gripped the poet. He drew back muttering in fear.

Into an enormous room. Grey.

Voices chattered. All alike.

"It's swell here," said a voice. "It isn't black as pitch."

"It isn't cold as ice," said another.

The poet's eyes snapped about in confused fury. He saw blurred forms, seated, standing, reclining. He backed into a gray wall.

"It isn't mean as sin," a voice said.

"It isn't raining cats and dogs," said another.

"Avaunt." The ancient lips framed automatically. "I say . . ."

"Gee whiz, but it's super dandy swell-elegant!" a voice cried happily.

The poet sobbed. He ran. "Surcease," he moaned. "Surcease."

"I'm in the plumbing game," said a man running beside him.

Iverson Lord gasped. He raced on, looking for escape.

"It's a rough game, the plumbing game," said the man.

A side hall. Iverson Lord plunged in frantically.

He ran past another room. He saw people cavorting around a gray maypole.

"By George!" they cried in ecstasy. "Great Guns! Holy Mackerel! Jiminy Cricket!"

The scholar clapped gaunt hands over his ears. He hurled himself on, driven.

Now, as he ran, there started in his ears a murmuring. A chorusing.

"A Stitch In Time Saves Nine. Time And Tide Wait For No Man." They chanted. "Early To Bed, Early To Rise. Too Many Cooks Spoil The Broth."

Iverson Lord cried out. "Gods of moulded symbol! *Pity!*"

The chorus hallelujahed. "Oh Boy!" they sang. "Wow! Gee Whiz! Hot Stuff!" Their voices swelled into a mighty "Land O' Goshen!"

"Aaaaah!" howled the poet. He flung himself against

a gray wall and clung there while the voices surrounded like melodic fog.

"Oh, my God," he rasped. "This is complete, this is unmitigated hell!"

"YOU SAID IT!" paeaned the chorus of thousands. "AIN'T IT THE TRUTH! OH WELL, YOU CAN'T LIVE FOREVER! THAT'S THE WAY IT GOES! HERE TODAY AND GONE TOMORROW! THAT'S LIFE!"

In four part harmony.

THE WEDDING

Then he told her they couldn't be married on Thursday because that was the day the Devil married his own mother.

They were at a cocktail party and she wasn't sure what he'd said because the room was noisy and she was a little high.

"What, darlin'?" she asked, leaning over to hear.

He told her again in his serious straightforward manner. She straightened up and smiled.

"Honest, you're a card," she said, and took a healthy sip from her Manhattan.

Later, while he was driving her home, she started talking about the day they were going to get married.

He said they'd have to change it: any day was all right except Thursday.

"I don't get you, darlin'." She put her head on his unbroad and sloping shoulder.

"Any day is all right except Thursday," he repeated.

She looked up, half the amusement dying hard. "All right hon," she said. "A joke's a joke."

"Who's joking?" he inquired.

She stared at him. "Darlin', are you crazy?"

He said, "No."

"But—you mean you want to change the date because . . . ?" She looked flabbergasted. Then she burst into a giggle and punched him on the arm. "You're a card, Frank," she said. "You had me goin' for a minute."

His small mouth pushed together into an irked bow.

"Dearest, I will not marry you on Thursday."

Her mouth fell open. She blinked. "My God, you're serious."

"Perfectly," he answered.

"Yeah, but . . ." she began. She chewed her lower lip. "You're crazy," she said, "because . . ."

"Look, is it so important?" he asked. "Why can't it be another day?"

"But you didn't say anythin' when we made the date," she argued.

"I didn't realize it was to be a Thursday."

She tried hard to understand. She thought he must have a secret reason. B.O. Bad breath. Something important. "But we made the date already," she offered weakly.

"I'm sorry." He was adamant. "Thursday is *out*."

She looked at him carefully. "Let's get this straight, Frank. You won't marry me on that Thursday?"

"Not on *any* Thursday."

"Well, I'm trying to understand, darlin'. But I'm damned if I can."

He didn't say anything.

Her voice rose. "You're bein' childish!"

"No, I'm not."

She slid away from him on the seat and glared out the window. "I'd like to know what *you* call it then."

She lowered the pitch of her voice to imitate his.

"I won't marry on Thursday because . . . because the Devil married his—grandmother or something."

"His mother," he corrected.

She snapped an irritated glance at him and clenched her fists.

"Make it another day and we'll forget the whole thing," he suggested.

"Oh sure. *Sure*," she said. "Forget the whole thing. Forget that my fiancé is afraid he'll make the Devil mad if he marries me on a Thursday. That's easy to forget."

"It's nothing to get excited about, dearest."

She groaned. "Oh! If you aren't the . . . the absolute limit."

She turned and looked at him. Her eyes narrowed suspiciously.

"How about Wednesday?" she asked.

He was silent. Then he cleared his throat with embarrassment.

"I—" he started, and then smiled awkwardly. "I forgot that, dear," he said. "Not Wednesday either."

She felt dizzy. "Why?" she asked.

"If we married on Wednesday, I'd be a cuckold."

She leaned forward to stare at him. "You'd be a *what?*" she asked in a shrill voice.

"A cuckold. You'd be unfaithful."

Her face contorted in shock.

"I—I," she spluttered. "Oh, *God*, take me home! I wouldn't marry you if you were the last man in the world!"

He kept driving carefully. She couldn't stand the silence.

She glared at him accusingly. "And—and I suppose if we got married on a-a *Sunday*, you'd turn into a pumpkin!"

"Sunday would be fine," he said.

"Oh, I'm so glad for you," she snapped. "You don't know how happy you've made me."

She turned away from him.

"Maybe you just don't *want* to marry me," she said. "Well, if you don't, *say so!* Don't give me all this crap about . . ."

"I want to marry you. You know that. But it has to be the right way. For both our sakes."

She hadn't intended to invite him in. But she was so used to his coming in that she forgot when they arrived at the house.

"You want a drink?" she asked sullenly as they went into the living room.

"No, thank you. I'd like to talk this thing over with you, sweetheart," he said, pointing to the couch.

She set down her chubby body stiffly. He took her hand.

"Dearest, please try to understand," he said.

He slid an arm around her and stroked her shoulder.

In another moment she melted. She looked into his face earnestly. "Darlin'," she said, "I want to understand. But how can I?"

He patted her shoulder. "Now listen, I just know certain things. And I believe that to marry on the wrong day would be fatal to our relationship."

"But . . . why?"

He swallowed. "Because of consequences."

She didn't say anything. She slid her arms around him and pressed close. He was too comfortable not to marry just because he wouldn't marry on Thursday. Or Wednesday.

She sighed. "All right, darlin'. We'll change it to Sunday. Will that make you happy?"

"Yes," he said. "That will make me happy."

. . .

Then one night he offered her father fifteen dollars to seal the bargain of their marriage.

Mr. O'Shea looked up from his pipe with an inquiring smile.

"Would you say that again?" he asked politely.

Frank held out the money. "I wish to pay this as purchase money for your daughter."

"Purchase money?" asked Mr. O'Shea.

"Yes, purchase."

"Who's sellin' her?" Mr. O'Shea inquired. "I'm givin' her hand in marriage."

"I know that," said Frank. "This is just symbolic."

"Put it in your hope chest," said Mr. O'Shea. He went back to his paper.

"I'm sorry, sir, but you must accept it," Frank insisted.

Then she came downstairs.

Mr. O'Shea looked at his daughter.

"Tell your young man to stop kiddin'," he said.

She looked at Frank with a worried glance. "Aw, you're not startin' in again, Frank."

Frank explained it to both of them. He made it clear that he in no way regarded her as a mere cash purchase;

that it was only the principle of the thing he wished to adhere to for both their sakes.

"All you have to do is take the money," he finished, "and everything will be all right."

She looked at her father. Her father looked at her.

"Take it, father," she sighed.

Mr. O'Shea shrugged and took the money.

"Four-nine-two," sang Frank. "Three-five-seven . . . eight-one-six. Fifteen, fifteen and thrice on my breast I spit to guard me safe from fascinating charms."

"Frank!" she cried. "You got your shirt all wet!"

Then he told her that, instead of throwing out her bouquet, she'd have to let all the men make a rush for her garter.

She squinted at him. "Come *on*, Frank. This is goin' too far."

He looked pained.

"I'm only trying to make things right for us," he said. "I don't want anything to go wrong."

"But—good God, Frank!—haven't you done enough? You got me to change the wedding day. You *bought* me for fifteen dollars and spit all over yourself in front of

Daddy. You make me wear this awful itchy hair bracelet. Well, I stood for it all. But I'm gettin' a little tired of it all. Enough's enough."

Frank got sad. He stroked her hand and looked like Joan of Arc going up in flames.

"I'm only trying to do what I think is best," he said. "We are beset by a host of dangers. We must be wary of what we do or all is lost."

She stared at him. "Frank, you *do* want to marry me, don't you? This isn't just a scheme to—?"

He swept her into his arms and kissed her fervently.

"Fulvia," he said, "*Dearest.* I love you and I want to marry you. But we must do what is right."

Later Mr. O'Shea said, "He's a jerk. Kick him out on his ear."

But she was rather chubby and she wasn't very pretty and Frank was the only man who'd ever proposed to her.

So she sighed and gave in. She talked it over with her mother and her father. She said that everything would be all right as soon as they got married. She said, "I'll humor him until then, and then—*whammo!*"

But she managed to talk him out of having the male wedding guests make a rush for her garter.

"You don't want me to get my neck broken, do you?" she asked.

"You're right," he said. "Just throw them your stockings."

"Darlin', let me throw my bouquet. Please?"

He looked pensive.

"All right," he said. "But I don't like it. I don't like it one bit."

He got some salt and put it in the hot oven in her kitchen. After a while he looked in.

"Now our tears are dry and we're all right for a while," he said.

The wedding day arrived.

Frank was up bright and early. He went to church and made sure all the windows were closed tight to keep the demons out. He told the pastor it was lucky it was February so the doors could be kept closed. He made it quite clear that no one was to be allowed to touch the doors during the ceremony.

The pastor got mad when Frank fired his .38 up the chimney.

"What in heaven's name are you doing!" he asked.

"I am just frightening off evil spirits," said Frank.

"Young man, there are no evil spirits in the First Calvary Episcopal Church!"

Frank apologized. But, while the pastor was out in the lobby explaining the shot to a local policeman, Frank took some dishes out of his overcoat pocket, broke them and put the pieces under pew seats and in corners.

Then he rushed downtown and bought twenty-five pounds of rice in case anyone ran out of it or forgot to bring it.

Hurrying back to his betrothed's house, he rang the bell.

Mrs. O'Shea answered. Frank asked, "Where's your daughter?"

"You can't see her now," Mrs. O'Shea said.

"I simply must," Frank demanded. He rushed past Mrs. O'Shea and dashed up the stairs.

He found his bride sitting on the bed in her petticoat polishing the shoes she was going to wear.

She jumped up. "What's the matter with you!" she cried.

"Give me one of your shoes," he gasped. "I almost forgot. It would have been doom if I'd forgotten."

He reached for a shoe. She drew back.

"Get out of here!" she cried, pulling on her bathrobe.

"Give me a shoe!"

She said, "No. What am I supposed to wear? Galoshes?"

"All right," he said, plunged into her closet and came out with an old shoe.

"I'll take this," he said and ran from the room.

She remembered something and her wail followed him out. "You aren't supposed to see me before we get married!"

"That's just a silly superstition!" he called back as he jumped down the staircase.

In the kitchen he handed the shoe to Mr. O'Shea who was sipping coffee and smoking his pipe.

"Give it to me," said Frank.

Mr. O'Shea said, "I'd like to."

Frank was oblivious. "Hand the shoe to me and say 'I transfer authority,'" he said.

Mr. O'Shea's mouth fell open. He took the shoe and handed it back dumbly.

"I transfer authority," he said.

Then he blinked. "Hey, wait!"

But Frank was gone. He jumped back upstairs.

"No!" she yelled as he ran into her room again. "Get the hell out of here!"

He hit her on the head with the shoe. She howled. He swept her into his arms and kissed her violently.

"My dearest wife," he said and ran out.

She burst into tears. "No, I'm *not* going to marry him!" She threw the polished shoes at the wall. "I don't care if he's the last man in the world. He's awful!"

After a while she picked up the shoes and polished them again.

About then Frank was downtown making sure the caterer had used exactly the right ingredients in the cake. Then he bought Fulvia a paper hat to wear when she ran from the church to the sedan. He went to every second hand store in town and bought all the old shoes he could to use as a defense against malign spirits.

By the time the wedding hour came he was exhausted.

He sat in the church anteroom, panting, running over the list he'd made to make sure nothing had been forgotten.

The organ started to play. And she came down the aisle with her father. Frank stood looking at her, still breathing quite heavily.

Then his eyebrows flew up as he noticed that a late-comer was just entering the front door.

"Oh, no!" he cried, covering his face with his hands. "I'm going to go up in a puff of smoke!"

But he didn't.

When he opened his eyes, his bride was holding his hand tightly.

"You see, Frank," she comforted, "you were full of baloney all the time."

The ceremony was performed. And he was so numbed with surprise and shock and bewilderment that he forgot about shoes and bouquets and hats and rice and everything.

As they rode to the hotel in the hired limousine, she stroked his hand.

"Superstition," she cooed. "It's the bunk."

"But—" Frank offered.

"Shush," she said, pressing shut his protest with a kiss. "Aren't you still alive?"

"Yes," said Frank, "and I can't understand it."

At the door to their hotel room Frank looked at her. She looked at him. The bellboy looked away.

Finally she said, "Carry me across the threshold, darlin'."

He smiled a flimsy smile.

"I'd feel silly about it," he said.

"For me," she insisted. "I'm entitled to *one* superstition."

He smiled then. "Yes," he admitted and bent to pick her up.

They never made it. She was awfully chubby.

"Heart failure," said the doctor.

"*Satan*," breathed Fulvia, remaining in a mottled funk the ensuing ten years.

THE CONQUEROR

That afternoon in 1871, the stage to Grantville had only the two of us as passengers, rocking and swaying in its dusty, hot confines under the fiery Texas sun. The young man sat across from me, one palm braced against the hard, dry leather of the seat, the other holding on his lap a small black bag.

He was somewhere near nineteen or twenty. His build was almost delicate. He was dressed in checkered flannel and wore a dark tie with a stickpin in its center. You could tell he was a city boy.

From the time we'd left Austin two hours before, I had been wondering about the bag he carried so carefully in his lap. I noticed that his light-blue eyes kept gazing down at it. Every time they did, his thin-lipped mouth would twitch—whether toward a smile or a grimace I couldn't tell. Another black bag, slightly larger, was on the seat beside him, but to this he paid little attention.

I'm an old man, and while not usually garrulous, I guess I do like to seek out conversation. Just the same, I hadn't offered to speak in the time we'd been fellow passengers, and neither had he. For about an hour and a half I'd been trying to read the Austin paper, but now I laid it down beside me on the dusty seat. I glanced down again at the small bag and noted how tightly his slender fingers were clenched around the bone handle.

Frankly, I was curious. And maybe there was something in the young man's face that reminded me of Lew or Tylan—my sons. Anyhow, I picked up the newspaper and held it out to him.

"Care to read it?" I asked him above the din of the 24 pounding hoofs and the rattle and creak of the stage.

There was no smile on his face as he shook his head once. If anything, his mouth grew tighter until it was a line of almost bitter resolve. It is not often you see such an expression in the face of so young a man. It is too hard at that age to hold on to either bitterness or resolution, too easy to smile and laugh and soon forget the worst of evils. Maybe that was why the young man seemed so unusual to me.

"I'm through with it if you'd like," I said.

"No, thank you," he answered curtly.

"Interesting story here," I went on, unable to rein in a runaway tongue. "Some Mexican claims to have shot young Wesley Hardin."

The young man's eyes raised up a moment from his bag and looked at me intently. Then they lowered to the bag again.

"'Course I don't believe a word of it," I said. "The man's not born yet who'll put John Wesley away."

The young man did not choose to talk, I saw. I leaned back against the jolting seat and watched him as he studiously avoided my eyes.

Still I would not stop. What is this strange compulsion of old men to share themselves? Perhaps they fear to lose their last years in emptiness. "You must have gold in that bag," I said to him, "to guard it so zealously."

It was a smile he gave me now, though a mirthless one.

"No, not gold," the young man said, and as he finished saying so, I saw his lean throat move once nervously.

I smiled and struck in deeper the wedge of conversation.

"Going to Grantville?" I asked.

"Yes, I am," he said—and I suddenly knew from his voice that he was no Southern man.

I did not speak then. I turned my head away and looked out stiffly across the endless flat, watching through the choking haze of alkali dust, the bleached scrub which dotted the barren stretches. For a moment, I felt myself tightened with that rigidity we Southerners contracted in the presence of our conquerors.

But there is something stronger than pride, and that is loneliness. It was what made me look back to the young man and once more see in him something of my own two boys who gave their lives at Shiloh. I could not, deep in myself, hate the young man for being from a different part of our nation. Even then, imbued as I was with the stiff pride of the Confederate, I was not good at hating.

"Planning to live in Grantville?" I asked.

The young man's eyes glittered. "Just for a while," he said. His fingers grew yet tighter on the bag he held so firmly in his lap. Then he suddenly blurted, "You want to see what I have in—"

He stopped, his mouth tightening as if he were angry to have spoken.

I didn't know what to say to his impulsive, half-finished offer.

The young man very obviously clutched at my indecision and said, "Well, never mind—you wouldn't be interested."

And though I suppose I could have protested that I would, somehow I felt it would do no good.

The young man leaned back and braced himself again as the coach yawed up a rock-strewn incline. Hot, blunt waves of dust-laden wind poured through the open windows at my side. The young man had rolled down the curtains on his side shortly after we'd left Austin.

"Got business in our town?" I asked, after blowing dust from my nose and wiping it from around my eyes and mouth.

He leaned forward slightly. "You live in Grantville?" he asked loudly as overhead the driver, Jeb Knowles, shouted commands to his three teams and snapped the leather popper of his whip over their straining bodies.

I nodded. "Run a grocery there," I said, smiling at him. "Been visiting up North with my oldest—with my son."

He didn't seem to hear what I had said. Across his face a look as intent as any I have ever seen moved suddenly.

"Can you tell me something?" he began. "Who's the quickest pistolman in your town?"

The question startled me, because it seemed born of no idle curiosity. I could see that the young man was far more than ordinarily interested in my reply. His hands were clutching, bloodless, the handle of his small black bag.

"Pistolman?" I asked him.

"Yes. Who's the quickest in Grantville? Is it Hardin? Does he come there often? Or Longley? Do they come there?"

That was the moment I knew something was not quite right in that young man. For, when he spoke those words, his face was strained and eager beyond a natural eagerness.

"I'm afraid I don't know much about such things," I told him. "The town is rough enough; I'll be the first man to admit to that. But I go my own way and folks like me go theirs and we stay out of trouble."

"But what about Hardin?"

"I'm afraid I don't know about that either, young man," I said. "Though I do believe someone said he was in Kansas now."

The young man's face showed a keen and heartfelt disappointment.

"Oh," he said and sank back a little.

He looked up suddenly. "But there are pistolmen there," he said, "*dangerous* men?"

I looked at him for a moment, wishing, somehow, that I had kept to my paper and not let the garrulity of age get the better of me. "There are such men," I said stiffly, "wherever you look in our ravaged South."

"Is there a sheriff in Grantville?" the young man asked me then.

"There is," I said—but for some reason did not add that Sheriff Cleat was hardly more than a figurehead, a man who feared his own shadow and kept his appointment only because the county fathers were too far away to come and see for themselves what a futile job their appointee was doing.

I didn't tell the young man that. Vaguely uneasy, I told him nothing more at all and we were separated by silence again, me to my thoughts, he to his—whatever strange, twisted thoughts they were. He looked at his bag and fingered at the handle, and his narrow chest rose and fell with sudden lurches.

A creaking, a rattling, a blurred spinning of thick spokes. A shouting, a deafening clatter of hoofs in the dust. Over the far rise, the buildings of Grantville were clustered and waiting.

A young man was coming to town.

Grantville in the postwar period was typical of those Texas towns that struggled in the limbo between lawlessness and settlement. Into its dusty streets rode men tense with the anger of defeat. The very air seemed charged with their bitter resentments—resentments toward the occupying forces, toward the rabble-rousing carpetbaggers and, with that warped evaluation of the angry man, toward themselves and their own kind. Threatening death was everywhere, and the dust was often red with blood. In such a town I sold food to men who often died before their stomachs could digest it.

I did not see the young man for hours after Jeb braked up the stage before the Blue Buck Hotel. I saw him move across the ground and up the hotel porch steps, holding tightly to his two bags.

Then some old friends greeted me and I forgot him.

I chatted for a while and then I walked by the store. Things there were in good order. I commended Merton Winthrop, the young man I had entrusted the store to in my three weeks' absence, and then I went home, cleaned up, and put on fresh clothes.

I judge it was near four that afternoon when I pushed through the batwings of the Nellie Gold Saloon. I am not nor ever was a heavy drinking man, but I'd had for several years the pleasurable habit of sitting in the cool shadows of a corner table with a whiskey drink to sip. It was a way that I'd found for lingering over minutes.

That particular afternoon I had chatted for a while with George P. Shaughnessy, the afternoon bartender, then retired to my usual table to dream a few presupper dreams and listen to the idle buzz of conversations and the click of chips in the back-room poker game.

That was where I was when the young man entered.

In truth, when he first came in, I didn't recognize him. For what a strange, incredible altering in his dress and carriage! The city clothes were gone; instead of a flannel coat he wore a broadcloth shirt, pearl-buttoned; in place of flannel trousers there were dark, tight-fitting trousers whose calves plunged into glossy, high-heeled boots. On his head a broad-brimmed hat cast a shadow across his grimly set features.

His boot heels had clumped him almost to the bar before I recognized him, before I grew suddenly aware of what he had been keeping so guardedly in that small black bag.

Crossed on his narrow waist, riding low, a brace of gunbelts hung, sagging with the weight of two Colt .44s in their holsters.

I confess to staring at the transformation. Few men in Grantville wore two pistols, much less slender young city men just arrived in town.

In my mind, I heard again the questions he had put to me. I had to set my glass down for the sudden, un-accountable shaking of my hand.

The other customers of the Nellie Gold looked only briefly at the young man, then returned to their several attentions. George P. Shaughnessy looked up, smiling, gave the customary unnecessary wipe across the immac-ulate mahogany of the bar top, and asked the young man's pleasure.

"Whiskey," the young man said.

"Any special kind, now?" George asked.

"Any kind," the young man said, thumbing back his hat with studied carelessness.

It was when the amber fluid was almost to the glass top that the young man asked the question I had somehow known he would ask from the moment I had recognized him.

"Tell me, who's the quickest pistolman in town?"

George looked up. "I beg your pardon, mister?"

The young man repeated the question, his face emotionless.

"Now, what does a fine young fellow like you want to know that for?" George asked him in a fatherly way.

It was like the tightening of hide across a drum top the way the skin grew taut across the young man's cheeks.

"I asked you a question," he said with unpleasant flatness. "Answer it."

The two closest customers cut off their talking to observe. I felt my hands grow cold upon the table top. There was ruthlessness in the young man's voice.

But George's face still retained the bantering cast it almost always had.

"Are you going to answer my question?" the young

man said, drawing back his hands and tensing them with light suggestiveness along the bar edge.

"What's your name, son?" George asked.

The young man's mouth grew hard and his eyes went cold beneath the shadowing brim of his hat. Then a calculating smile played thinly on his lips. "My name is Riker," he said as if somehow he expected this unknown name to strike terror into all our hearts.

"Well, young Mr. Riker, may I ask you why you want to know about the quickest pistolman in town?"

"Who *is* it?" There was no smile on Riker's lips now; it had faded quickly into that grim, unyielding line again. In back I noticed one of the three poker players peering across the top of half-doors into the main saloon.

"Well, now," George said, smiling, "there's Sheriff Cleat. I'd say that he's about—"

His face went slack. A pistol was pointing at his chest.

"Don't tell me lies," young Riker said in tightly restrained anger. "I know your sheriff is a yellow dog; a man at the hotel told me so. I want the *truth*."

He emphasized the word again with a sudden thumbing back of hammer. George's face went white.

"Mr. Riker, you're making a very bad mistake," he

said, then twitched back as the long pistol barrel jabbed into his chest.

Riker's mouth was twisted with fury. "Are you going to *tell* me?" he raged. His young voice cracked in the middle of the sentence like an adolescent's.

"Selkirk," George said quickly.

The young man drew back his pistol, another smile trembling for a moment on his lips. He threw across a nervous glance at where I sat ~~but did~~ not recognize me. Then his cold blue eyes were on George again.

"Selkirk," he repeated. "What's the first name?"

"Barth," George told him, his voice having neither anger nor fear.

"Barth Selkirk." The young man spoke the name as though to fix it in his mind. Then he leaned forward quickly, his nostrils flaring, the thin line of his mouth once more grown rigid.

"You tell him I want to kill him," he said. "Tell him I—" He swallowed hastily and jammed his lips together. "Tonight," he said then. "Right here. At eight o'clock." He shoved out the pistol barrel again. "You *tell* him," he commanded.

George said nothing and Riker backed away from the bar, glancing over his shoulder once to see where the doors were. As he retreated, the high heel of his right boot gave a little inward and he almost fell. As he staggered for balance, his pistol barrel pointed restlessly around the room, and in the rising color of his face, his eyes looked with nervous apprehension into every dark corner.

Then he was at the doors again, his chest rising and falling rapidly. Before our blinking eyes, the pistol seemed to leap back into its holster. Young Riker smiled uncertainly, obviously desperate to convey the impression that he was in full command of the moment.

"Tell him I don't like him," he said as if he were tossing out a casual reason for his intention to kill Selkirk. He swallowed again, lowering his chin a trifle to hide the movement of his throat.

"Tell him he's a dirty Rebel," he said in a breathless-sounding voice. "Tell him—tell him I'm a Yankee and I *hate* all Rebels!"

For another moment he stood before us in wavering defiance. Then suddenly he was gone.

George broke the spell. We heard the clink of glass on glass as he poured himself a drink. We watched him swallow it in a single gulp. "Young fool," he muttered.

I got up and went over to him.

"How do you like *that?*" he asked me, gesturing one big hand in the general direction of the doors.

"What are you going to do?" I asked him, conscious of the two men now sauntering with affected carelessness for the doors.

"What am I *supposed* to do?" George asked me. "Tell Selkirk, I guess."

I told George about my talk with young Riker and of his strange transformation from city boy to, apparently, self-appointed pistol killer.

"Well," George said when I was finished talking, "where does that leave me? I can't have a young idiot like that angry with me. Do you know his triggers were filed to a hair? Did you see the way he slung that Colt?" he shook his head. "He's a fool," he said. "But a dangerous fool—one that a man can't let himself take chances with."

"Don't tell Selkirk," I said. "I'll go to the sheriff and—"

George waved an open palm at me. "Don't joke now, John," he said. "You know Cleat hides his head under the pillow when there's shooting in the air."

"But this would be a slaughter, George," I said. "Selkirk is a hardened killer, you know that for a fact."

George eyed me curiously. "Why are you concerned about it?" he asked me.

"Because he's a boy," I said. "Because he doesn't know what he's doing."

George shrugged. "The boy came in and asked for it himself, didn't he?" he said. "Besides, even if I say nothing, Selkirk will hear about it, you can be sure of that. Those two who just went out—don't you think *they'll* spread the word?"

A grim smile raised Shaughnessy's lips. "The boy will get his fight," he said. "And may the Lord have mercy on his soul."

George was right. Word of the young stranger's challenge flew about the town as if the wind had blown it. And with the word, the threadbare symbol of our justice, Sheriff Cleat, sought the sanctuary of his house, having either scoffed at all storm warnings or ignored them in his practiced way.

But the storm *was* coming; everyone knew it. The people who had found some reason to bring them to the square—they knew it. The men thronging the Nellie Gold who seemed to have developed a thirst quite out of keeping with their normal desires—they knew it. Death is a fascinating lure to men who can stand aside and watch it operate on someone else.

I stationed myself near the entrance of the Nellie Gold, hoping that I might speak to young Riker, who had been in his hotel room all afternoon, alone.

At seven-thirty, Selkirk and his ruffian friends galloped to the hitching rack, tied up their snorting mounts, and went into the saloon. I heard the greetings offered them and their returning laughs and shouts. They were elated, all of them; that was not hard to see. Things had been dull for them in the past few months. Cleat had offered no resistance, only smiling fatuously to their bullying insults. And, in the absence of any other man willing to draw his pistol on Barth Selkirk, the days had dragged for him and for his gang, who thrived on violence. Gambling and drinking and the company of Grantville's lost women was not enough for these men. It was why they were all bubbling with excited anticipation that night.

While I stood waiting on the wooden sidewalk, endlessly drawing out my pocket watch, I heard the men shouting back and forth among themselves inside the saloon. But the deep, measured voice of Barth Selkirk I did not hear. He did not shout or laugh then or ever. It was why he hovered like a menacing wraith across our town. For he spoke his frightening logic with the thunder of his pistols and all men knew it.

Time was passing. It was the first time in my life that impending death had taken on such immediacy to me. My boys had died a thousand miles from me, falling while, oblivious, I sold flour to the blacksmith's wife. My wife had died slowly, passing in the peace of slumber, without a cry or a sob.

Yet now I was deeply in this fearful moment. Because I had spoken to young Riker, because—yes, I knew it now—he had reminded me of Lew, I now stood shivering in the darkness, my hands clammy in my coat pockets, in my stomach a hardening knot of dread.

And then my watch read eight. I looked up—and I heard his boots clumping on the wood in even, unhurried strides.

I stepped out from the shadows and moved toward him. The people in the square had grown suddenly quiet. I sensed men's eyes on me as I walked toward Riker's approaching form. It was, I knew, the distortion of nerves and darkness, but he seemed taller than before as he walked along with measured steps, his small hands swinging tensely at his sides.

I stopped before him. For a moment, he looked irritably confused. Then that smile that showed no humor flickered on his tightly drawn face.

"It's the grocery man," he said, his voice dry and brittle.

I swallowed the cold tightness in my throat. "Son, you're making a mistake," I said, "a very bad mistake."

"Get out of my way," he told me curtly, his eyes glancing over my shoulder at the saloon.

"Son, *believe* me. Barth Selkirk is too much for you to—"

In the dull glowing of saloon light, the eyes he turned on me were the blue of frozen, lifeless things. My voice broke off, and without another word, I stepped aside to let him pass. When a man sees in another man's eyes the insensible determination that I saw in Riker's, it is best to step aside. There are no words that will affect such men.

A moment more he looked at me and then, squaring his shoulders, he started walking again. He did not stop until he stood before the batwings of the Nellie Gold.

I moved closer, staring at the light and shadows of his face illuminated by the inside lamps. And it seemed as though, for a moment, the mask of relentless cruelty fell from his features to reveal stark terror.

But it was only a moment, and I could not be certain I had really seen it. Abruptly, the eyes caught fire again, the thin mouth tightened, and Riker shoved through the doors with one long stride.

There was silence, utter ringing silence in that room. Even the scuffing of my bootheels sounded very loud as I edged cautiously to the doors.

Then, as I reached them, there was that sudden rustling, thumping, jingling combination of sounds that indicated general withdrawal from the two opposing men.

I looked in carefully.

Riker stood erect, his back to me, looking toward the bar. It now stood deserted save for one man.

Barth Selkirk was a tall man who looked even taller because of the black he wore. His hair was long and blond; it hung in thick ringlets beneath his wide-brimmed hat. He wore his pistol low on his right hip, the butt reversed, the holster thonged tightly to his thigh. His face was long and tanned, his eyes as sky-blue as Riker's, his mouth a motionless line beneath the well-trimmed length of his mustaches.

I had never seen Abilene's Hickok, but the word had always been that Selkirk might have been his twin.

As the two eyed each other, it was as though every watching man in that room had ceased to function, their breaths frozen, their bodies petrified—only their eyes alive, shifting back and forth from man to man. It might have been a room of statues, so silently did each man stand.

Then I saw Selkirk's broad chest slowly expanding as it filled with air. And as it slowly sank, his deep voice broke the silence with the impact of a hammer blow on glass.

"*Well?*" he said and let his boot slide off the brass rail and thump down onto the floor.

An instant pause. Then, suddenly, a gasping in that room as if one man had gasped instead of all.

For Selkirk's fingers, barely to the butt of his pistol, had turned to stone as he gaped dumbly at the brace of Colts in Riker's hands.

"Why you dirty—" he began—and then his voice was lost in the deafening roar of pistol fire. His body was flung back against the bar edge as if a club had struck him in the chest. He held there for a moment, his face blank with astonishment. Then the second pistol kicked thundering in Riker's hand and Selkirk went down in a twisted heap.

I looked dazedly at Selkirk's still body, staring at the great gush of blood from his torn chest. Then, my eyes were on Riker again as he stood veiled in acrid smoke before the staring men.

I heard him swallow convulsively. "My name is Riker," he said, his voice trembling in spite of efforts to control it. "Remember that. *Riker*."

He backed off nervously, his left pistol holstered in a blur of movement, his right still pointed toward the crowd of men.

Then he was out of the saloon again, his face contorted with a mixture of fear and exultation as he turned and saw me standing there.

"Did you see it?" he asked me in a shaking voice. "Did you *see* it?"

I looked at him without a word as his head jerked to the side and he looked into the saloon again, his hands plummeting down like shot birds to his pistol butts.

Apparently he saw no menace, for instantly his eyes were back on me again—excited, swollen-pupiled eyes.

"They won't forget me now, will they?" he said and

swallowed. "They'll remember my name. They'll be afraid of it."

He started to walk past me, then twitched to the side and leaned, with a sudden weakness, against the saloon wall, his chest heaving with breath, his blue eyes jumping around feverishly. He kept gasping at the air as if he were choking.

He swallowed with difficulty. "Did you *see* it?" he asked me again, as if he were desperate to share his murderous triumph. "He didn't even get to pull his pistols— didn't even get to *pull* them." His lean chest shuddered with turbulent breath. "*That's* how," he gasped, "*that's* how to do it." Another gasp. "I showed them. I showed them all how to do it. I came from the city and I showed them how. I got the best one they had, the *best one*." His throat moved so quickly it made a dry, clicking sound. "I showed them," he muttered.

He looked around blinking. "Now I'll—"

He looked all around with frightened eyes, as if an army of silent killers were encircling him. His face went slack and he forced together his shaking lips.

"Get out of my way," he suddenly ordered and pushed me aside. I turned and watched him walking rapidly toward the hotel, looking to the sides and over his shoulder with quick jerks of his head, his hands half poised at his sides.

I tried to understand young Riker, but I couldn't. He was from the city; that I knew. Some city in the mass of cities had borne him. He had come to Grantville with the deliberate intention of singling out the fastest pistolman and killing him face to face. That made no sense to me. That seemed a purposeless desire.

Now what would he do? He had told me he was only going to be in Grantville for a while. Now that Selkirk was dead, that while was over.

Where would young Riker go next? And would the same scenes repeat themselves in the next town, and the next, and the next after that? The young city man arriving, changing outfits, asking for the most dangerous pistolman, meeting him—was that how it was going to be in every town? How long could such insanity last? How long before he met a man who would not lose the draw?

My mind was filled with these questions. But, over all, the single question—*Why?* Why was he doing this thing? What calculating madness had driven him from the city to seek out death in this strange land?

While I stood there wondering, Barth Selkirk's men carried out the blood-soaked body of their slain god and laid him carefully across his horse. I was so close to them that I could see his blond hair ruffling slowly in the night wind and hear his life's blood spattering on the darkness of the street.

Then I saw the six men looking toward the Blue Buck Hotel, their eyes glinting vengefully in the light from the Nellie Gold, and I heard their voices talking low. No words came clear to me as they murmured among themselves, but from the way they kept looking toward the hotel I knew of what they spoke.

I drew back into the shadows again, thinking they might see me and carry their conversation elsewhere. I stood in the blackness watching. Somehow I knew exactly what they intended even before one of their shadowy group slapped a palm against his pistol butt and said distinctly, "*Come on.*"

I saw them move away slowly, the six of them, their voices suddenly stilled, their eyes directed at the hotel they were walking toward.

Foolishness again; it is an old man's trademark. For, suddenly, I found myself stepping from the shadows and turning the corner of the saloon, then running down the alley between the Nellie Gold and Pike's Saddlery; rushing through the squares of light made by the saloon windows, then into darkness again. I had no idea why I was running. I seemed driven by an unseen force which clutched all reason from my mind but one thought— *warn him.*

My breath was quickly lost. I felt my coattails flapping like furious bird wings against my legs. Each thudding bootfall drove a mail-gloved fist against my heart.

I don't know how I beat them there, except that they were walking cautiously while I ran headlong along St. Vera street and hurried in the backway of the hotel. I rushed down the silent hallway, my bootheels thumping along the frayed rug.

Maxwell Tarrant was at the desk that night. He looked up with a start as I came running up to him.

"Why, Mr. Callaway," he said, "what are—?"

"Which room is Riker in?" I gasped.

"Riker?" young Tarrant asked me.

"*Quickly*, boy!" I cried and cast a frightened glance toward the entranceway as the jar of bootheels sounded on the porch steps.

"Room 27," young Tarrant said. I begged him to stall

the men who were coming in for Riker, and rushed for the stairs.

I was barely to the second floor when I heard them in the lobby. I ran down the dimlit hall, and reaching Room 27, I rapped urgently on its thin door.

Inside, I heard a rustling sound, the sound of stock-inged feet padding on the floor, then Riker's frail, trembling voice asking who it was.

"It's Callaway," I said, "the grocery man. Let me in, quickly. You're in danger."

"Get out of here," he ordered me, his voice sounding thinner yet.

"God help you, boy, prepare yourself," I told him breathlessly. "Selkirk's men are coming for you."

I heard his sharp, involuntary gasp. "*No*," he said. "That isn't—" He drew in a rasping breath. "How *many?*" he asked me hollowly.

"Six," I said, and on the other side of the door I thought I heard a sob.

"That isn't fair!" he burst out then in angry fright. "It's not fair, six against one. It isn't *fair!*"

I stood there for another moment, staring at the door, imagining that twisted young man on the other side, sick with terror, his heart jolting like club beats in his chest, able to think of nothing but a moral quality those six men never knew.

"What am I going to *do?*" he suddenly implored me.

I had no answer. For, suddenly, I heard the thumping of their boots as they started up the stairs, and helpless in my age, I backed quickly from the door and scuttled, like the frightened thing I was, down the hall into the shadows there.

Like a dream it was, seeing those six grim-faced men come moving down the hall with a heavy trudging of boots, a thin jingling of spur rowels, in each of their hands a long Colt pistol. No, like a nightmare, not a dream. Knowing that these living creatures were headed for the room in which young Riker waited, I felt something sinking in my stomach, something cold and wrenching at my insides. Helpless I was; I never knew such helplessness. For no seeming reason, I suddenly saw my Lew inside that room, waiting to be killed. I made me tremble without the strength to stop.

Their boots halted. The six men ringed the door, three on one side, three on the other. Six young men, their faces tight with unyielding intention, their hands bloodless, so tightly did they hold their pistols.

The silence broke. "Come out of that room, you Yan-

kee bastard!" one of them said loudly. He was Thomas
Ashwood, a boy I'd once seen playing children's games in
the streets of Grantville, a boy who had grown into the
twisted man who now stood, gun in hand, all thoughts
driven from his mind but thoughts of killing and re-
venge.

Silence for a moment.

"I said, *come out!*" Ashwood cried again, then jerked
his body to the side as the hotel seemed to tremble with a
deafening blast and one of the door panels exploded into
jagged splinters.

As the slug gouged into papered plaster across the hall,
Ashwood fired his pistol twice into the door lock, the
double flash of light splashing up his cheeks like light-
ning. My ears rang with the explosions as they echoed
up and down the hall.

Another pistol shot roared inside the room. Ashwood
kicked in the lock-splintered door and leaped out of my
sight. The ear-shattering exchange of shots seemed to
pin me to the wall.

Then, in a sudden silence, I heard young Riker cry
out in a pitiful voice, "Don't shoot me any more!"

The next explosion hit me like a man's boot kicking at my stomach. I twitched back against the wall, my breath silenced, as I watched the other men run into the room and heard the crashing of their pistol fire.

It was over—all of it—in less than a minute. While I leaned weakly against the wall, hardly able to stand, my throat dry and tight, I saw two of Selkirk's men help the wounded Ashwood down the hall, the other three walking behind, murmuring excitedly among themselves. One of them said, "We got him good."

In a moment, the sound of their boots was gone and I stood alone in the empty hallway, staring blankly at the mist of powder smoke that drifted slowly from the open room.

I do not remember how long I stood there, my stomach a grinding twist of sickness, my hands trembling and cold at my sides.

Only when young Tarrant appeared, white-faced and frightened at the head of the steps, did I find the strength to shuffle down the hall to Riker's room.

We found him lying in his blood, his pain-shocked eyes staring sightlessly at the ceiling, the two pistols still smoking in his rigid hands.

He was dressed in checkered flannel again, in white

shirt and dark stockings. It was grotesque to see him lying there that way, his city clothes covered with blood, those long pistols in his still, white hands.

"Oh, God," young Tarrant said in a shocked whisper. "Why did they kill him?"

I shook my head and said nothing. I told young Tarrant to get the undertaker and said I would pay the costs. He was glad to leave.

I sat down on the bed, feeling very tired. I looked into young Riker's open bag and saw, inside, the shirts and underclothes, the ties and stockings.

It was in the bag I found the clippings and the diary.

The clippings were from Northern magazines and newspapers. They were about Hickok and Longley and Hardin and other famous pistol fighters of our territory. There were pencil marks drawn beneath certain sentences—such as *Wild Bill usually carries two derringers beneath his coat* and *Many a man has lost his life because of Hardin's so-called "border roll" trick.*

The diary completed the picture. It told of a twisted mind holding up as idols those men whose only talent was to kill. It told of a young city boy who bought himself pistols and practiced drawing them from their holsters until he was incredibly quick, until his drawing speed became coupled with an ability to strike any target instantly.

It told of a projected odyssey in which a city boy would make himself the most famous pistol fighter in the Southwest. It listed towns that this young man had meant to conquer.

Grantville was the first town on the list.

DEAR DIARY

June 10, 1954
Dear Diary:

Honest, sometimes I get so sick of this damn furnished room I could absolutely vomit!

The window is so dirty—half the time on Saturday and Sunday mornings I think it's going to rain even if the sun is shining.

And such a view! Underwear yet, dripping on wash

lines. Girdles, overalls. If it isn't enough to make a girl wish she was dead. It all stinks.

And that jiboney across the hall. He makes life worse than it is. Where he gets his money for booze, who knows? Probably he robs old ladies. Drunk—sings all the time, makes lunges at me in that hallway that looks like a dungeon hall in an Errol Flynn picture. For two cents—less—I'd send to the mail order factory for a thirty-two caliber pistol. Then I'd shoot the crumb. They'd put me away, no more worries. Aaah, it ain't worth it.

And what jolly joy is tomorrow night. Harry Hartley takes me to the Paramount and for one lousy show and a cheap chow mein feed he wants I should play wife to him all night. Honest, men!

Honest, it's so stinking hot.

Now I have to wash out some stuff for tomorrow. I hate to think about it. Oh, shut up! Those dumb dopes across the way—jabber, jabber! New York Giants, Brooklyn Dodgers—they should all drop dead!

And when I think of that lousy subway ride tomorrow—twice! Those bodies like sardines, the faces popping like roses. Some pleasure!

God, what I wouldn't do to get away from this. I'd

even marry Harry Hartley and if I'd do that, I know things are bad.

Oh, to go to Hollywood and be a star like Ava Gardner or them. Having the men fall all over themselves to kiss your hand. Go away, Clark, you bother me. Yeah, he should bother me. I'd crawl all over him.

Oooh, this lousy, stinking place! A girl hasn't no future here. What can I look forward to? No guy who likes me except that fat dope. Chow Mein Harry I think I'll call him.

Vacation in two weeks. Two weeks of nothing. Go to Coney with Gladys. Sit on the damn beach and look at the garbage float on the water and go crazy watching kids neck themselves blind. Then I get all sun-burned and maybe a fever even. And I go to a million movies. It's some life.

I wish it was a couple of thousand years from now, that's what I wish. Then—no work. I live in a fancy spot and they have rocket ships and you can eat pills for a meal and free love. Would I go for that! The pills, of course. Like fun!

This isn't no time to be living. Wars, people yelling at each other and what can a girl expect out of life?

Oh, I've got to wash my lousy underwear.

June 10, 3954
Dear Factum:

Sometimes—yes!—I become so ill of this cursed plastoid dwelling that I could be inclined toward regurgitation.

What a dismal view!

The spaceport across the highway. All night—*buzz, buzz*—and those red shooting exhausts from the vents. Even taking the pills and rubbing narcotilotion on my eyes and ears doesn't help. It is all quite sufficient to make me ill. It is all very foul.

And that idiot neighbor with his ray machine. It infuriates me to know that he can see through the plastoid. Even when I put up my fibre screen I feel him staring. Where does he get the purchase tickets for his invention materials? His job at the spaceport doesn't pay enough. I dare say he steals exchange tickets from the business office.

For two minimatickets I'd get myself an atomizer gun from the spaceport armory and decompose the damned lecher! Then they'd put me away in the Venus pits and I'd be all set.

No, it isn't worth it. I can't stand heat and I loathe sand storms.

And tomorrow night—oh, foul joy—Hendrick Halley takes me to the Space Theatre and for one wretched performance and a dull meal of fricaseed lunar bat he expects me to undergo the risk of impregnation. Honestly, men.

Oh, it's so dreadfully warm. And my fool electro washer has to be misaligned just when I need it. I'll have to fly down to the Spaceomat to wash my clothes and I do so weary of night flying.

Oh, there they go again—those fools across the way. Why don't they turn off their speakers? This damned local board has to know every word we say. There they go again! Martian Eagles, Lunar Red Sox—may they all succumb to a vacuum.

And when I think of that miserable spaceship ride tomorrow—twice! That lumbering monstrosity. Imagine— more than an *hour* to Mars for heaven's sake!

Oh, it's too much. What I wouldn't do to get away from it all. I'd even undergo a societal juncture with Hendrick Halley. Great galaxies, things can't be *that* advanced!

Oh, to go to the theatre capital and be a notable like Gell Fig or someone like her. To have all the men swooning and begging you to fly with them to their country planets. I do loathe this shiny spotless city.

Oh, this vile spot! What future has a young woman here? None. I have no man who appeals—certainly not lunar bat Halley with his nasty little ship that has rusty seams. I wouldn't even trust that wreck on a hop to Europa.

Vacationing in two weeks. Nothing to do. Dull trip to The Moon Resort. Sitting by that godawful pool and watching the young people pleasure themselves. And then I get that red dust in my nostrils and get a fever. And a million trips to the Space Theatre. Oh, how pitiful.

I wish it were the olden days, many thousands of years ago. Then a person could know what was what. There was so much to do. Men were men and not the bald, toothless idiots they are now.

I could do much as I pleased without the government checking my every step.

This is no time to be alive. What can a young woman like myself expect in these times?

Oh, curses. I must fly down to the Spaceomat and get my clothes done.

XXXX
Dear Slab:

Sometimes I get so sick of this damn cave I could . . .

DESCENT

It was impulse, Les pulled the car over to the curb and stopped it. He twisted the shiny key and the motor stopped. He turned to look across Sunset Boulevard, across the green hills that dropped away steeply to the ocean.

"Look, Ruth," he said.

It was late afternoon. Far out across the palisades they could see the Pacific shimmering with reflections of the red sun. The sky was a tapestry dripping gold and crimson. Streamers of billowy, pink-edged clouds hung across it.

"It's so pretty," Ruth said.

His hand lifted from the car seat to cover hers. She smiled at him a moment, then the smile faded as they watched the sunset again.

"It's hard to believe," Ruth said.

"What?" he asked.

"That we'll never see another."

He looked soberly at the brightly colored sky. Then he smiled but not in pleasure.

"Didn't we read that they'd have artificial sunsets?" he said. "You'll look out the windows of your room and see a sunset. Didn't we read that somewhere?"

"It won't be the same," she said, "will it, Les?"

"How could it be?"

"I wonder," she murmured, "what it will be really like."

"A lot of people would like to know," he said.

They sat in silence watching the sun go down. It's funny he thought, you try to get underneath to the real meaning of a moment like this but you can't. It passes and when it's over you don't know or feel any more than you did before. It's just one more moment added to the past. You *don't* appreciate what you have until it's taken away.

He looked over at Ruth and saw her looking solemnly and strangely at the ocean.

"Honey," he said quietly and gave her, with the word, his love.

She looked at him and tried to smile.

"We'll still be together," he told her.

"I know," she said. "Don't pay any attention to me."

"But I will," he said, leaning over to kiss her cheek. "I'll look after you. Over the earth—"

"Or under it," she said.

Bill came out of the house to meet them. Les looked at his friend as he steered the car into the open concrete space by the garage. He wondered how Bill felt about leaving the house he'd just finished paying for. Free and clear, after eighteen years of payments, and tomorrow it would be rubble. Life is a bastard, he thought, switching off the engine.

"Hello, kid," Bill said to him. "Hi, beautiful," to Ruth.

"Hello, handsome," Ruth said.

They got out of the car and Ruth took the package off the front seat. Bill's daughter Jeannie came running out of the house. "Hi, Les! Hi, Ruth!"

"Say, Bill, whose car are we going to take tomorrow?" Les asked him.

"I don't know, kid," Bill said. "We'll talk it over when Fred and Grace get here."

"Carry me piggy-back, Les," Jeannie demanded.

He swung her up. *I'm glad we don't have a child, I'd hate to take a child down there tomorrow.*

Mary looked up from the stove as they moved in. They all said hello and Ruth put the package on the table.

"What's that?" Mary asked.

"I baked a pie," Ruth told her.

"Oh, you didn't have to do that," Mary said.

"Why not? It may be the last one I'll ever bake."

"It's not that bad," Bill said. "They'll have stoves down there."

"There'll be so much rationing it won't be worth the effort," Ruth said.

"The way my true love bakes that'll be good fortune," Bill said.

"Is *that* so!" Mary glared at her grinning husband,

who patted her behind and moved into the living room with Les. Ruth stayed in the kitchen to help.

Les put down Bill's daughter.

Jeannie ran out. "Mama, I'm gonna help you make dinner!"

"How nice," they heard Mary say.

Les sank down on the big cherry-colored couch and Bill took the chair across the room by the window.

"You come up through Santa Monica?" he asked.

"No, we came along the Coast Highway," Les said. "Why?"

"Jesus, you should have gone through Santa Monica," Bill said. "Everybody's going crazy—breaking store windows, turning cars upside down, setting fire to everything. I was down there this morning. I'm lucky I got the car back. Some jokers wanted to roll it down Wilshire Boulevard."

"What's the matter, are they crazy?" Les said. "You'd think this was the end of the world."

"For some people it is," Bill said. "What do you think MGM is going to do down there, make cartoons?"

"Sure," said Les. "*Tom and Jerry in the Middle of the Earth.*"

Bill shook his head. "Business is going out of its mind," he said. "There's no place to set up everything down there. Everybody's flipping. Look at that paper."

Les leaned forward and took the newspaper off the coffee table. It was three days old. The main stories, of course, covered the details of the descent—the entry schedules at the various entrances: the one in Hollywood, the one in Reseda, the one in downtown Los Angeles. In large type across eight columns, the frontpage headline read: REMEMBER! THE BOMB FALLS AT SUNSET! Newspapers had been carrying the warning for a week. And tomorrow was the day.

The rest of the stories were about robbery, rape, arson, and murder.

"People just can't take it," Bill said. "They have to flip."

"Sometimes I feel like flipping myself," said Les.

"Why?" Bill said with a shrug. "So we live under the ground instead of over it. What the hell will change? Television will still be lousy."

"Don't tell me we aren't even leaving that above ground?"

"No, didn't you see?" Bill said. He pushed up and walked over to the coffee table. He picked up the paper

Les had dropped. "Where the hell is it?" he muttered to himself, ruffling through the pages.

"There." Bill held out the paper.

TELEVISION TO GO ON
SCIENTISTS PROMISE

"Consolation?" Les said.

"Sure," Bill said, tossing down the paper. "Now we'll be able to watch the bomb smear us."

He went back to his chair.

Les shook his head. "Who's going to build television sets down there?"

"Kid, there'll be everything down—what's up, beautiful?"

Ruth stood in the archway that opened on the living room.

"Anybody want wine?" she asked. "Beer?"

Bill said beer and Les said wine, then Bill went on.

"Maybe that promise of television is a little far-fetched," he said. "But, otherwise, there'll be business as usual. Oh, maybe it'll be on a different level, but it'll be there. Christ, somebody's gonna want something for all the money they've invested in the Tunnels."

"Isn't their life enough?"

Bill went on talking about what he'd read concerning life in the Tunnel—the exchange set-up, the transportation system, the plans for substitute food production and all the endless skein of details that went into the creation of a new society in a new world.

Les didn't listen. He sat looking past his friend at the purple and red sky that topped the shifting dark blue of the ocean. He heard the steady flow of Bill's words without their content; he heard the women moving in the kitchen. What *would* it be like?—he wondered. Nothing like this. No aquamarine broadloom, wall to wall, no vivid colors, no fireplace with copper screening, most of all no picture windows with the beautiful world outside for them to watch. He felt his throat tighten slowly. Tomorrow and tomorrow and tomorrow—

Ruth came in with the glasses and handed Bill his beer and Les his wine. Her eyes met those of her husband for a moment and she smiled. He wanted to pull her down suddenly and bury his face in her hair. He wanted to forget. But she returned to the kitchen and he said "What?" to Bill's question.

"I said I guess we'll go to the Reseda entrance."

"I guess it's as good as any other," Les said.

"Well, I figure the Hollywood and the downtown entrances will be jammed," Bill said. "Christ, you really threw down that wine."

Les felt the slow warmth run down into his stomach as he put down the glass.

"This thing getting you, kid?" Bill asked.

"Isn't it getting you?"

"Oh . . ." Bill shrugged. "Who knows? Maybe I just make noise to hide what it's doing to me. I guess. I feel it for Jeannie more than anything else. She's only five."

Outside they heard a car pull up in front of the house and Mary called to say that Fred and Grace were there. Bill pressed palms on his knees and pushed up.

"Don't let it get you," he said with a grin. "You're from New York. It won't be any different from the subway."

Les made a sound of disgruntled amusement.

"Forty years in the subway," he said.

"It's not that bad," Bill said, starting out of the room. "The scientists claim they'll find some way to de-radiate the country and get things growing again."

"When?"

"Maybe twenty years," Bill said, and then he went out to welcome his guests.

"But how do we know what they *really* look like?"

Grace said. "All the pictures they print are only artist's *conceptions* of what the living quarters are like down there. They may be *holes* in the wall for all we know."

"Don't be a knocker, kid, be a booster," Bill told her.

"Uh!" Grace grunted. "I think you're oblivious to the—*terror* of this horrible descent into the ground."

They were all in the living room full of steak and salad and biscuits and pie and coffee. Les sat on the cherry-colored couch, his arm round Ruth's slender waist. Grace and Fred sat on the yellow studio couch, Mary and Bill in separate chairs. Jeannie was in bed. Warmth filtered from the fireplace where a low, steady log fire burned. Fred and Bill drank beer from cans and the rest drank wine.

"Not oblivious, kid," Bill said. "Just adjusting. We have to do it. We might as well make the best of it."

"Easily said, easily said," Grace repeated. "But I for one *certainly* don't look forward to living in those tunnels. I expect to be miserable. I don't know how Fred feels, but those are *my* sentiments. I don't think it really *matters* to Fred."

"Fred is an adjuster," Bill said. "Fred is not a knocker."

Fred smiled a little and said nothing. He was a small man sitting by his wife like a patient boy with his mother in the dentist's office.

"Oh!" Grace again. "How can you be so blasé about it is beyond me. How can it be *anything* but bad? No theatres, no restaurants, no travelling—"

"No beauty parlors," said Bill with a short laugh.

"*Yes*, no beauty parlors," said Grace. "If you don't think *that's* important to a woman—*well*."

"We'll have our loved ones," Mary said. "I think that's most important. And we'll be alive."

Grace shrugged. "All right we'll be alive, we'll be together," she said. "But I'm afraid I just can't call that life—living in a *cellar* the rest of my life."

"Don't go," Bill said. "Show 'em how tough you are."

"*Very* funny," Grace said.

"I bet some people *will* decide not to go down there," Les said.

"If they're *crazy*," said Grace. "Uh! What a *hideous* way to die."

"Maybe it's better than going underground," Bill said. "Who knows? Maybe a lot of people will spend a quiet day at home tomorrow."

"*Quiet?*" said Grace. "Don't worry, Fred and I will be down in those tunnels bright and early tomorrow."

"I'm not worried," said Bill.

They were quiet for a moment, then Bill said, "The

Reseda entrance all right with everybody? We might as well decide now."

Fred made a small palms-up gesture with his hands.

"All right with me," he said. "Whatever the majority decides."

"Kid, let's face it," Bill said. "You're the most important person we've got here. An electrician's going to be a big man down there."

Fred smiled. "That's okay," he said. "Anything you decide."

"You know," Bill said. "I wonder what the hell we mailmen are going to do down there."

"And we bank tellers," Les said.

"Oh, there'll be money down there," Bill said. "Where America goes, money goes. Now what about the car? We can only take one for six. Shall we take mine? It's the biggest."

"Why not *ours?*" Grace said.

"Doesn't matter a damn to me," Bill said. "We can't take them down with us anyway."

Grace stared bitterly at the fire, her frail hands opening and closing in her lap.

"Oh, why don't we *stop* the bomb! Why don't we attack *first?*"

"We can't stop it now," Les said.

"I wonder if they have tunnels too," said Mary.

"Sure," Bill said. "They're probably sitting in their houses right now just like us, drinking wine and wondering what'll it be like to go underground."

"Not *them*," Grace said, bitterly. "What do *they* care?"

Bill smiled dryly. "They care."

"There doesn't seem any point," Ruth said.

Then they all at in silence watching their last fire of a cool California evening. Ruth rested her head on Les's shoulder as he slowly stroked her blonde hair. Bill and Mary caught each other's eye and smiled a little. Fred sat and stared with gentle, melancholy eyes at the glowing logs while Grace opened up and closed her hands and looked very old.

And, outside, the stars shone down for a million times the millionth year.

Ruth and Les were sitting on their living room floor listening to records when Bill sounded his horn. For a moment they looked at each other without a word, a little frightened, the sunlight filtering between the blinds and falling like golden ladders across their legs. What can

I say?—he wondered suddenly—Are there any words in the world that can make this minute easier for her?

Ruth moved against him quickly and they clung together as hard as they could. Outside the horn blew again.

"We'd better go," Les said quietly.

"All right," she said.

They stood up and Les went to the front door.

"We'll be right out!" he called.

Ruth moved into the bedroom and got their coats and the two small suitcases they were allowed to take. All their furniture, their clothes, their books, their records—they had to be left behind.

When she went back to the living room, Les was turning off the record player.

"I wish we could take more books," he said.

"They'll have libraries, honey," she said.

"I know," he said. "It just—isn't the same."

He helped her on with her coat and she helped him on with his. The apartment was very quiet and warm.

"It's so nice," she said.

He looked at her a moment as if in question, then, hurriedly, he picked up the suitcases and opened the door.

"Come on, baby," he said.

At the door she turned and looked back. Abruptly she walked over to the record player and turned it on. She stood there emotionlessly until the music sounded, then she went back to the door and closed it firmly behind them.

"Why did you do that?" Les asked.

She took his arm and they started down the path to the car.

"I don't know," she said, "maybe I just want to leave our home as if it were alive."

A soft breeze blew against them as they walked and, overhead, palm trees swayed their ponderous leaves.

"It's a nice day," she said.

"Yes, it is," he said and her fingers tightened on his arm.

Bill opened the door for them.

"Hop in, kids," he said. "And we'll get rolling."

Jeannie got on her knees on the front seat and talked to Les and Ruth as the car started up the street. Ruth turned and watched the apartment house disappear.

"I felt the same way about our house," Mary said.

"Don't fret, Ma," Bill said. "We'll make out down thar."

"What's *down thar?*" Jeannie asked.

"God knows," said Bill, then, "Daddy's joking, baby. Down thar means down *there*."

"Say, Bill, do you think we'll be living near each other in The Tunnels?" Les asked.

"I don't know, kid," Bill said. "It goes by district. *We'll* be pretty close together I guess, but Fred and Grace won't, living way the hell over in Venice the way they do."

"I can't say I'm sorry," Mary said. "I don't relish the idea of listening to Grace complain for the next twenty years."

"Oh, Grace is all right," Bill said. "All she needs is a good swift kick where it counts once in a while."

Traffic was heavy on the main boulevards that ran east for the two city entrances. Bill drove slowly along Lincoln Boulevard towards Venice. Outside of Jeannie's chattering none of them spoke. Ruth and Les sat close to each other, hands clasped, eyes straight ahead. Today, the words kept running through his mind: *we're going underground, we're going underground today.*

At first nothing happened when Bill honked the horn. Then the front door of the little house jerked open and Grace came running wildly across the broad lawn, still wearing her dressing gown and slippers, her gray-black hair hanging down in long braids.

"Oh my God, what's happened?" Mary said as Bill pushed quickly from the car to meet Grace. He pulled open the gate in time to catch Grace as one of her slipper heels dug into the soft earth throwing her off balance.

"What's *wrong?*" he asked, bracing her with his hands.

"It's *Fred!*" she cried.

Bill's face went blank and his gaze jumped suddenly to the house standing silent and white in the sunshine. Les and Mary got out of the car quickly.

"What's wrong with—" Bill started, cutting off his words nervously.

"He won't go!" Grace cried, her face a mask of twisted fright.

They found him as Grace said he'd been all morning—fists clenched, sitting motionless in his easy chair by the window that overlooked the garden. Bill walked over to him and laid a hand on his thin shoulder.

"What's up, buddy?" he asked.

Fred looked up, a smile starting at the corners of his small mouth. "Hi," he said quietly.

"You're not going?" Bill asked.

Fred took a breath and seemed about to say something

else, then he stopped. "No," he said as if he were politely refusing peas at dinner.

"Oh, my God, I *told* you, I *told* you!" Grace sobbed. "He's *insane!*"

"All right, Grace, *take it easy.*" Bill snapped irritably and she pressed the soaked handkerchief to her mouth. Mary put her arm around Grace.

"Why not, pal?" Bill asked his friend.

Another smile twitched momentarily on Fred's lips. He shrugged slightly.

"Don't want to," he said.

"Oh, Fred, Fred, how can you *do* this to me?" Grace moaned, standing nervously by the front door, right hand to her throat. Bill's mouth tightened but he kept his eyes on Fred's motionless face.

"What about Grace?" he asked.

"Grace should go," Fred answered. "I want her to go, I don't want her to die."

"How can I live down there *alone?*" Grace sobbed.

Fred didn't answer, he just sat there looking straight ahead as if he felt embarrassed by all this attention, as if he was trying to gather in his mind the right thing to say.

"Look," he started, "I know this is terrible and—and it's arrogant—but I just can't go down there."

His mouth grew firm. "I won't," he said.

Bill straightened up with a weary breath.

"Well," he said hopelessly.

"I—" Fred had opened up his right fist and was uncrumpling a small square of paper. "Maybe—this will say—say what I mean."

Bill took it and read it. Then he looked down at Fred and patted his shoulder once.

"Okay, pal," he said and he put the paper in his coat. He looked at Grace.

"Get dressed if you're coming," he said.

"*Fred!*" she almost screamed his name. "Are you going to *do* this terrible thing to me?"

"Your husband is staying," Bill told her. "Do you want to stay with him?"

"I don't want to *die!*"

Bill looked at her a moment, then turned away.

"Mary, help her dress," he said.

While they went to the car, Grace sobbing and stumbling on Mary's arm, Fred stood in the front doorway and watched his wife leave. She hadn't kissed him or embraced him, only retreated from his goodbye with a sob of angry fear. He stood there without moving a muscle and the breeze ruffled his thin hair.

When they were all in the car Bill took the paper out of his pocket.

"I'm going to read you what your husband wrote," he said flatly and he read: "*If a man dies with the sun in his eyes, he dies a man. If a man goes with dirt on his nose—he only dies.*"

Grace looked at Bill with bleak eyes, her hands twisting endlessly in her lap.

"Mama, why isn't Uncle Fred coming?" Jeannie asked as Bill started the car and made a sharp U-turn.

"He wants to stay," was all Mary said.

The car picked up speed and headed toward Lincoln Boulevard. None of them spoke and Les thought of Fred sitting back there alone in his little house, waiting. *Alone.* The thought made his throat catch and he gritted his teeth. Was there another poem beginning in Fred's mind now, he thought, one that started—*If a man dies and there is no one there to hold his hand—*

"Oh, *stop* it, stop the car!" Grace cried.

Bill pulled over to the curb.

"I don't want to go down there alone," Grace said miserably. "It's not fair to make me go alone. I—"

She stopped talking and bit her lip. "Oh—" She leaned over. "Goodbye, Mary," she said and she kissed her. "Goodbye, Ruth," and kissed her. Then Les and Jeannie, and she managed a brief, rueful smile at Bill.

"I hate you," she said.

"I *love* you," he answered.

They watched her go back down the block, first walking, then, as she got nearer to the house, half running with a childlike excitement. They saw Fred come to the gate and then Bill started the car and he drove away and they were alone together.

"You'd never think Fred felt that way, would you?" Les said.

"I don't know, kid," Bill said. "He always used to stay in his garden when he wasn't working. He liked to wear a pair of shorts and a T-shirt and let the sun fall on him while he trimmed the hedges or mowed the lawn or something. I can understand him feeling the way he does. If he wants to die that way, why not? He's old enough to know what he wants." He grinned. "It's Grace that surprises me."

"Don't you think it was a little unfair of him sort of—*pushing* Grace into staying with him?" Ruth asked.

"What's fair or unfair?" Bill said. "It's a man's life and a man's love. Where's the book that tells a man how to die and how to love?"

He turned the car onto Lincoln Boulevard.

They reached the entrance a little after noon and one of the hundreds in the concentrated police force directed them to the field down the road and told them to park there and walk back.

"Jesus, would you look at those cars," Bill said as he drove slowly along the road that was thick with walking people.

Cars, thousands of them. Les thought of the field he'd seen once after WWII. It had been filled with bombers, wing to wing as far as the eye could see. This was just like it, only these were cars and the war wasn't over, it was just beginning.

"Isn't it dangerous to leave all the cars here?" Ruth asked. "Won't it make a target?"

"Kid, no matter where the bomb falls it's going to smear everything," Bill said.

"Besides," said Les, "the way the entrances are built I don't think it matters much where the bomb lands."

They all got out and stood for a moment as if they weren't sure exactly what to do. Then Bill said, "Well, let's go," and patted the hood of his car. "So long, clunk—RIP."

"In pieces?" Les said.

There were long lines at each of the twenty desks before the entrance. People filed slowly by and gave their names and addresses and were assigned to various bunker rows. They didn't talk much, they just held their suitcases and moved along with little steps towards the entrance to The Tunnels.

Ruth held Les's arm with clenched fingers and he felt a tautness growing around the edges of his stomach, as if the muscles there were slowly calcifying. Each short, undramatic step took them closer to the entrance, further from the sky and the sun and the stars and the moon. And suddenly Les felt very sick and afraid. He wanted to grab Ruth's hand and drive back to their apartment and stay there till it ended. Fred was right—he couldn't help feeling it. Fred was right to know that a man couldn't leave the only home he'd ever had and burrow into the earth like a mole and still be himself. Something would happen down there, something would change. The artificial air, the even banks of bulbed sunshine, the electric moon and the fluorescent stars invented at the behest of some psychological study that foretold aberration if they were taken away completely. Did they suppose these things would be enough? Could they possibly believe that a man might crawl beneath the ground in one great living grave for twenty years and keep his soul?

He felt his body tighten involuntarily and he wanted to scream out at all the stupidity in the world that made men scourge themselves to their own destruction. His breath caught and he glanced at Ruth and he saw that she was looking at him.

"Are you all right?"

He drew in a shaking breath. "Yes," he said. "All right."

He tried to numb his mind but without success. He kept looking at all the people around him, wondering if they felt, as he did, this fierce anger at what was happening, at what, basically, they had allowed to happen. Did they think too of the night before, of the stars and the crisp air and sounds of earth? He shook his head. It was torture to think about them.

He looked over at Bill as the five of them shuffled slowly down the long concrete ramp to the elevators. Bill was holding Jeannie's hand in his, looking down at her without any expression on his face. Then Les saw him turn and nudge Mary with the suitcase he held in his other hand. Mary looked at him and Bill winked.

"Where are we going, Papa?" Jeannie asked, and her voice echoed shrilly off the white tile walls.

Bill's throat moved. "I told you," he replied. "We're going to live under the ground a while."

"How long?" Jeannie asked.

"Don't talk anymore, baby," Bill said. "I don't know."

There was no sound in the elevator. There were a hundred people in it and it was as still as a tomb as it went down. And down. And down.

THE DOLL THAT DOES EVERYTHING

The poet screamed, "Devil spawn! Scrabbling lizard! Maniacal kangaroo!"

His scraggy frame went leaping through the doorway, then locked into paralysis. "*Fiend!*" he gagged.

The object of this mottled-faced abuse squatted oblivious in a snowbank of confettied manuscript. Manuscript delivered of sweaty gestation, typewritten in quivering agony.

"Foaming moonstruck *octopus!* Shovel-handed *ape!*" The blood-laced eyes of Ruthlen Beauson bagged gibbously behind their horn-rimmed lenses. At hipless sides, his fingers shook like leprous stringbeans in a gale. Ulcers within ulcers throbbed.

"*Hun!*" he raged anew, "*Goth! Apache!* Demented nihilist!"

Saliva dribbling from his teething maw, little Gardner Beauson bestowed a one-toothed grin upon his palsied sire. Shredded poetry filtered through his stubby fists as the semi-spheroid of his bottom hovered dampishly above each lacerated amphibrach with iambic variation.

Ruthlen Beauson groaned a soul-wracked groan. "*Confusion,*" he lamented in a trembling voice. "Untrammeled farrago."

Then, suddenly, his eyes embossed into metallic orbs, his fingers petrified into a strangler's pose. "I'll do him in," he gibbered faintly, "I'll snap his hyoid with a brace of thumbs."

Upon this juncture, Athene Beauson, smock bespattered, hands adrip with soppy clay, swept into the room like a wraith of vengeance resurrected from the mud.

"What *now?*" she asked, acidulous through gritted teeth.

"Look! *Look!*" Ruthlen Beauson's forefinger jabbed fitfully as he pointed toward their sniggering child. "He's destroyed my *Songs of Sconce!*" His 20-90 eyes went bulgy mad. "I'll carve him," he foreboded in a roupy whisper, "I'll *carve* the shriveled viper!"

"Oh . . . *look out*," Athene commanded, pulling back her butcher-bent spouse and dragging up her son by his drool-soaked undershirt.

Suspended over heaps of riven muse, he eyed his mother with a saucy aspect.

"*Whelp!*" she snapped, then let him have one, soundly, on his bulbous rump.

Gardner Beauson screeched in inflammatory protest, was shown the door and exited, his little brain already cocked for further action. A residue of clay upon his diaper, he waddled, saucer-eyed, into the plenitude of breakables which was the living room as Athene turned to see her husband on his knees, aghast, in the rubble of a decade's labor.

"I shall destroy myself," the poet mumbled, sagging shouldered. "I'll inject my veins with lethal juices."

"Get up, get up," said Athene crisply, face a sour mask.

Ruthlen floundered to his feet. "I'll kill him, yes, I'll kill the wizened beast," he said in hollow-hearted shock.

"That's *no* solution," said his wife. "Even though . . ."

Her eyes grew soft a moment as she dreamed of

nudging Gardner into a vat of alligators. Her full lips quivered on the brink of tremulous smiling.

Then her green eyes flinted. "That's *no* solution," she repeated, "and it's time we solved this goddamn thing."

Ruthlen stared with dumb-struck eyes upon the ruins of his composition. "I'll kill him," he divulged to the scattered fragments, "I'll—"

"Ruthlen, *listen* to me," said his wife, clay-soaked fingers clenching into fists.

His spiritless gaze lifted for a moment.

"Gardner needs a playmate," she declared. "I read it in a book. He needs a playmate."

"I'll kill him," mumbled Ruthlen.

"Will you *listen!*"

"Kill him."

"I tell you Gardner has to have a playmate! I don't care whether we can afford it or not, he needs a playmate!"

"Kill," the poet hissed. "Kill."

"I don't care if we haven't got a cent! You want time for poetry and I want time for sculpting!"

"My *Songs of Sconce.*"

"*Ruthlen Beauson!*" Athene screamed, a moment's time before the deafening shatter of a vase.

"Good God, what *now!*" Athene exclaimed.

They found him dangling from the mantelpiece, cater-wauling for succor and immediate change of diaper . . .

THE DOLL THAT DOES EVERYTHING!

Athene stood before the plate glass window, lips pursed in deep deliberation. In her mind, a vivid balance see-sawed—grave necessity on the one side, sterile income on the other. Implastic contemplation ridged her brow. They had no money, that was patent. Nursery school was out, a governess impossible. And yet, there had to be an answer; there *had* to be.

Athene braced herself and strode into the shop.

The man looked up, a kindly smile dimpling his apple cheeks, welcoming his customer.

"That doll," Athenes inquired. "Does it really do the things your placard says it does?"

"That doll," the salesman beamed, "is quite without comparison, the nonpareil of toycraft. It walks, it talks, it eats and drinks, dispenses body wastes, snores while it sleeps, dances a jig, rides a seesaw and sings the choruses of seven childhood favorites." He caught his breath. "To name a few," he said, "it sings 'Molly Andrews'—"

"What is the cost of—"

"It swims the crawl for fifty feet, it reads a book, plays thirteen simple etudes on the pianoforte, mows the lawn, changes its own diapers, climbs a tree and burps."

"What is the price of—"

"And it grows," the salesman said.

"It . . ."

"*Grows*," the man reiterated, slit-eyed. "Within its plastic body are all the cells and protoplasms necessary for a cycle of maturation lasting up to twenty years."

Athene gaped.

"At one-thousand-oh-seven-fifty, an obvious bargain," the man concluded. "Shall I have it wrapped or would you rather walk it home?"

A swarm of eager hornets, each a thought, buzzed inside the head of Athene Beauson. It was the perfect playmate for little Gardner. One-thousand-seven-fifty though! Ruthlen's scream would shatter windows when he saw the tag.

"You can't go wrong," the salesman said.

He *needs* a playmate!

"Time payments can easily be arranged." The salesman guessed her plight and fired his *coup de grâce*.

All thoughts disappeared like chips swept off a gambling table. Athene's eyes caught fire; a sudden smile pulled up her lip ends.

"A boy doll," she requested eagerly. "One year old."

The salesman hurried to his shelves . . .

No windows broke but Athene's ears rang for half an hour after.

"Are you *mad?*" her husband's scream had plunged its strident blades into her brain. "*One-thousand-seven-fifty!*"

"We can pay on time."

"With *what?*" he shrieked. "Rejection slips and *clay!*"

"Would you rather," Athene lashed out, "have your son alone all day? Wandering through the house—*tearing— cracking—ripping—crushing?*"

Ruthlen winced at every word as if they were spiked shillelagh blows crushing in his head. His eyes fell shut behind the quarter-inch lenses. He shuddered fitfully.

"Enough," he muttered, pale hand raised, surrendering. "Enough, *enough.*"

"Let's bring the doll to Gardner," Athene said excitedly.

They hurried to the little bedroom of their son and

found him tearing down the curtains. A hissing, taut-cheeked Ruthlen jerked him off the window sill and knuckle-rapped him on the skull. Gardner blinked once his beady eyes.

"Put him down," Athene said quickly. "Let him see."

Gardner stared with one-toothed mouth ajar at the little doll that stood so silently before him. The doll was just about his size, dark-haired, blue-eyed, flesh-colored, diapered, exactly like a real boy.

He blinked furiously.

"Activate the mechanism," Ruthlen whispered and Athene, leaning over, pushed the tiny button.

Gardner toppled back in drooling consternation as the little boy doll grinned at him. "Bah-bi-bah-bah!" Gardner cried hysterically.

"Bah-bi-bah-bah," echoed the doll.

Gardner scuttled back, wild-eyed, and, from a wary crouch, observed the little boy doll waddling toward him. Restrained from further retreat by the wall, he cringed with tense astonishment until the doll clicked to a halt before him.

"Bah-bi-bah-bah." The boy doll grinned again, then burped a single time and started in to jig on the linoleum.

Gardner's pudgy lips spread out, abruptly, in an idiotic grin. He gurgled happily. His parents' eyes went shut as one, beatific smiles creasing their grateful faces, all thoughts of financial caviling vanished.

"*Oh*," Athene whispered wonderingly.

"I can't believe it's true," her husband said, guttural with awe . . .

For weeks, they were inseparable, Gardner and his motor-driven friend. They squatted down together, exchanging moon-eyed glances, chuckling over intimate jollities and, in general, relishing to the full their drooly *tête à têtes*. Whatever Gardner did, the doll did too.

As for Ruthlen and Athene, they rejoiced in this advent of near-forgotten peace. Nerve-knotting screams no longer hammered malleus on incus and the sound of breaking things was not upon the air. Ruthlen poesied and Athene sculpted, all in a bliss of sabbath privacy.

"You see?" she said across the dinner table of an evening. "It was all he needed; a companion," and Ruthlen bowed his head in solemn tribute to his wife's perspicacity.

"True, 'tis true," he whispered happily.

A week, a month. Then gradually, the metamorphosis.

Ruthlen, bogged in sticky pentameter, looked up one morning, eyes marbleized. "Hark," he murmured.

The sound of dismemberment of plaything.

Ruthlen hastened to the nursery to find his only be-gotten ripping cotton entrails from a heretofore respected doll.

The gloom-eyed poet stood outside the room, his heartbeat dwindling to the sickening thud of old while, in the nursery, Gardner disemboweled and the doll sat on the floor, observing.

"No," the poet murmured, sensing it was yes. He crept away, somehow managing to convince himself it was an accident.

However, early the following afternoon at lunch, the fingers of both Ruthlen and his wife pressed in so sharply on their sandwiches that slices of tomato popped across the air and into the coffee.

"What," said Athene horribly, "is that?"

Gardner and his doll were found ensconced in the rubble of what had been, in happier times, a potted plant.

The doll was watching with a glassy interest as Gard-ner heaved up palmfuls of the blackish earth which rained in dirty crumbs upon the rug.

"No," the poet said, ulcers revivified and, "No," the echo fell from Athene's paling lips.

Their son was spanked and put to bed, the doll was

barricaded in the closet. A wounded caterwauling in their ears, the wife and husband twitched through wordless lunch while acids bred viler acids in their spasmed stomachs.

One remark alone was spoken as they faltered to their separate works and Athene said it.

"It was an accident."

But, in the following week, they had to leave their work exactly eighty-seven times.

Once it was Gardner thrashing in pulled-down draperies in the living room. Another time it was Gardner playing piano with a hammer in response to the doll's performance of a Bach gavotte. Still another time and time after time it was a rash of knocked-down objects ranging from jam jars to chairs. In all, thirty breakables broke, the cat disappeared and the floor showed through the carpet where Gardner had been active with scissors.

At the end of two days, the Beausons poesied and sculpted with eyes embossed and white lips rigid over grinding teeth. At the end of four, their bodies underwent a petrifying process, their brains began to ossify. By the week's end, after many a flirt and flutter of their viscera, they sat or stood in palsied silence, waiting for new outrages and dreaming of violent infanticide.

The end arrived.

One evening, suppering on a pitcherful of stomach-easing seltzers, Athene and her husband sat like rigor-mortised scarecrows in their chairs, their eyes four balls of blood-threaded stupor.

"What are we to do?" a spirit-broken Ruthlen muttered.

Athene's head moved side to side in negating jerks. "I thought the doll—" she started, then allowed her voice to drift away.

"The doll has done no good," lamented Ruthlen. "We're right back where we started. And deeper still by one-thousand-seven-fifty, since you say the doll cannot be exchanged."

"It can't," said Athene. "It's—"

She was caught in mid-word by the noise.

It was a moist and slapping sound like someone heaving mud against a wall. Mud or—

"No." Athene raised her soul-bruised eyes. "Oh, no."

The sudden spastic flopping of her sandals on the floor syncopated with the blood-wild pounding of her heart. Her husband followed on his broomstick legs, lips a trembling circle of misgiving.

"*My figure!*" Athene screamed, standing a stricken

marble in the studio doorway, staring ashen-faced upon the ghastly sight.

Gardner and the doll were playing *Hit the Roses on the Wallpaper*, using for ammunition great doughy blobs of clay ripped from Athene's uncompleted statue.

Athene and Ruthlen stood in horror-struck dumbness staring at the doll who, in the metal doming of its skull had fashioned new synaptic joinings and, to the jigging and the climbing and the burping, added flinging of clay.

And, suddenly it was clear—the falling plant, the broken vases and jars on high shelves—*Gardner needed help for things like that!*

Ruthlen Beauson seered a grisly future; i.e., the grisly past times two; all the Guignol torments of living with Gardner but multiplied by the presence of the doll.

"Get that metal monster from this house," Ruthlen mumbled to his wife through concrete lips.

"But there's no exchange!" she cried hysterically.

"Then it's me for the can opener!" the poet rasped, backing away on rocklike legs.

"It's not the doll's fault!" Athene shouted. "What good will tearing up the doll do? It's *Gardner*. It's that horrid thing we made together!"

The poet's eyes clicked sharply in their sockets as he

looked from doll to son and back again and knew the hideous truth of her remark. It was their son. The doll just imitated, the doll would do whatever it was—

—*made to do.*

Which was, precisely, to the second, when the idea came and, with it, peace unto the Beauson household.

From the next day forth, their Gardner—once more alone—was a model of deportment, the house became a sanctuary for blessed creation.

Everything was perfect.

It was only twenty years later, when a college-going Gardner Beauson met a wriggly sophomore and blew thirteen gaskets and his generator that the ugly truth came out.

THE TRAVELLER

Silent snows descended like a white curtain as Professor Paul Jairus hurried under the dim archway and onto the bare campus of Fort College.

His rubber-protected shoes squished aside the thin slush as he walked. He raised the collar of his heavy overcoat almost to the brim of his pulled down fedora. Then he drove his hands back into his coat pockets and clenched them into fists of chilled flesh.

He strode as rapidly as he could without getting the

icy slush on his trousers and ankles. Clouds of steam puffed from his lips as he pressed on. He looked up a moment at the high granite face of the Physical Sciences Center far across the wide campus. Then he lowered his almost colorless face to avoid the cutting wind and hurried on around the curving path, his feet carrying him past the line of skeletal trees whose branches stood brittle and black in the freezing air.

The wind seemed to push him back from his destination. It almost seemed to Jairus as if it were battling him. But that was pure imagination, of course. Keen desire to be over the preliminary steps only made them seem harder. He *was* anxious. In spite of endless self-examination and preparation, the thought of what he was soon to witness excited him. Far beyond the power of wind to chill or snow to whiten.

Or mind to caution.

Now he was past the edge of the huge building. It shielded Jairus from the wind and he raised his dark eyes. In his pockets, his hands flexed impatiently and he felt a strong inclination to break into a run. He must watch himself. If he appeared too excitable they might change their minds about letting him go. They had responsibilities, after all. He took a deep breath and let the cold air into his lungs. Once the initial fascination had gone he'd be his old rational self. It was the uniqueness of the situation that was upsetting his usual balance. But it was ridiculous to be *this* anxious.

He pushed through the revolving door into the building and almost sighed with pleasure as the warm air rushed over him. He took off his hat and shook the drops onto the marble floor. Then he unbuttoned his coat as he turned right and started down the long hallway. His rubbers squeaked as he walked.

To think, the idea probed at his brain, in less than a half hour it will happen. He shook his head at the inexplicable import of it . . . Never mind, he told himself, control yourself, that's all. You'll need self control to resist the pummeling of false sentiment.

Near the end of the hall he stopped in front of a door, half blond wood, half frosted glass. His eyes moved briefly over the printed words before he pushed in.

DR. PHILLIPS. DR. RANDALL. A blank space, recently scratched out. And, underneath, in neat red letters, the word:

CHRONO-TRANSPOSITION.

. . .

"You understand clearly then," said Dr. Phillips in an urgent voice, "you are to make no attempt to affect your surroundings in any way."

Jairus nodded.

"We have to emphasize that," Dr. Randall spoke from his chair. "It's the essential point. Any physical imposition on your surroundings might be fatal to yourself. And . . ." He gestured. ". . . to our program."

"I quite understand," Jairus said. "You can depend on my discretion."

Randall nodded once. He held up his hands and drew the fingers together nervously. "I suppose you know about Wade," he said.

"I've heard rumors," Jairus replied. "But nothing specific."

"Professor Wade was lost in the last transposition," Dr. Phillips said soberly. "The chamber returned without him. We must assume he is dead."

"That was early in September," Randall said. "It's taken us over two months to convince the board to let us try again. If we fail this time . . . well, that's the end of it."

"I see," Jairus said.

"I hope you do, professor, I hope you do," Dr. Phillips broke in. "A great deal is at stake."

"Well, let's not depress him anymore," Randall said with a tired smile. "I think you also know you're about to see something a lot of people would willingly give their lives to see."

"I know it," Jairus said. I also know a lot of people are fools, he thought.

"Shall we go then?" Randall asked.

The footsteps of the three men echoed in the hallway as they walked toward the Apparatus Laboratory. Jairus kept his hands in his coat pockets and did not speak except to make brief replies to their questions. Randall was telling him about the time screen.

"We've discarded the chamber as a dangerous vehicle for travel," Randall said. "You will travel in a circular energy screen which will render you invisible to the people you'll see. The screen *can* be broken by you but I think we've made it clear how perilous that can be."

"You will *please* remain within the screen boundaries," Phillips emphasized. "You must understand that."

"Yes," Jairus said. "I understand it."

"As an added measure, though," Randall said, "you will communicate with us through a chest speaker. This will give us information as you see it. And, also, if you feel any uneasiness, any premonition of danger to yourself—why, you have only to tell us and we'll bring you back immediately. At any rate your . . . *visit*, shall we say, will not exceed one hour."

An hour, Jairus thought. More than enough time to dispel the fallacies of the ages.

"With your health, your education, your background," Randall was saying, "you should have no difficulties."

"One thing I've wondered," Jairus said. "What makes you pick out this particular event instead of any other?"

Randall shrugged. "Maybe because it's almost Christmas."

Sentimental rot, Jairus thought.

They pushed through the heavy metal doors in the Apparatus Laboratory and Jairus saw graduate students moving around a metal platform set on conductor bars arranged like ties. The white-frocked students were setting up and adjusting what appeared to be colored spotlights all pointed to one spot on the platform.

Phillips went into the control room and Randall led Jairus to the platform and introduced him to the students. Then he checked the platform and the lights while Jairus stood by, nervous in spite of self-regimentation, heartbeats trembling his lean body.

Watch it now, he told himself, no emotional involvement. There, that's better. This is exciting, yes, but only as a scientific accomplishment, remember. The wonder is in the visiting and not the moment I am to visit. Years of study have made that quite clear. It's nothing.

That's what he kept telling himself as he stood there on the platform, his hands shaking, watching the lab disappear as though it were blotted away. Feeling his heart pound violently and being unable to stop the pounding with rational words. Words that were: it's nothing, *nothing.* It's only an execution, only an execution, only . . .

I'm standing on Golgotha.

It's about nine o'clock in the morning. The skies are clear. There are no clouds, the sun is bright. This place, the so-called place of the skull, is a bare, unvegetated eminence about a half mile from the walls of Jerusalem. The hill is to the northwest of the city on a high, uneven plain which extends between the walls of the city and the two valleys of Kedron and Hinnom.

It's a very depressing location. Something akin to an unkempt city lot in our own times. From where I stand

I can see discarded garbage and even animal excrement. A few dogs are foraging in the garbage. Quite depressing.

The hill is deserted except for two Roman soldiers. They're putting the upright stakes into the ground, hammering them with mallets into the holes they've dug. Looking around I can see a few people straggling up the hill. Apparently they want to get a good spot to watch the execution. You always find those kind of people, I guess.

It's warm here. I can feel the heat through the screen. The smell too. It's most offensive. There are large flies around. They move in and out of the energy screen without seeming to be blocked. I suppose that means people will do the same.

THAT'S CORRECT, PROFESSOR.

Wait. I can see a cloud of dust. A procession is coming this way. About ten to fifteen soldiers, I'd judge. And there are three men. Two quite burly ones in the lead. In the rear is a . . . is *him*. He's . . . oh, the dust is hiding him.

The two soldiers here are finished with their stakes. They're putting on their armor. Now they're buckling on their swords. One of the people asks them how soon it will start. The soldier says soon enough. Now they're . . .

. . . .

SOMETHING WRONG?

No, no, I'm just watching. I'm sorry. I should be talking. It's a little hard to remember.

Well, *apparently*, the legend about Simon of Cyrene is factual. The last man . . . *him*, dropped to the earth on his knees. Those cross beams . . . they must weigh almost two hundred pounds. The man can't get up. Now the soldiers are beating him. He can't rise. Too weak, I guess. Some other soldiers are forcing a passerby to lift the cross beam from the man's shoulders. The man stands. He follows behind Simon. I'll assume it's Simon of Cyrene. It can't be proved, of course.

Now the procession is quite close. I can see the two thieves. They're large men, hairy armed with long, dirty robes on their bodies. They don't seem to be having any trouble with their burdens. One of them is even laughing, it appears. Yes, he *is*. He just said something to one of the soldiers and the soldier laughed too.

They're almost here. I can . . .

I can see Jesus.

He's bent over but I can see he's quite tall. Over six feet I'd say. But he's quite thin. He's obviously been fasting. His face and hands are almost white from dust. He's stumbling. He just coughed from the dust in his lungs. His robe is dirty too. There are stains on it. Apparently . . . they've been throwing dung at him.

His face is without expression. Very stolid. His eyes look lifeless. He stares ahead of himself as he moves on. His beard is uncombed and tangled, so is his hair. He looks as if he's half dead already. As a matter of fact he looks . . . quite *ordinary*. Yes he . . .

. . . .

PROFESSOR JAIRUS?

They're here now. I'm standing about seven yards away from the stakes. I can see the three men quite clearly. I can even see the wounds around the head of Jesus. Again I can only assume. That the wounds were made by a crown of thorns, I mean. One can't be sure. The gouges appear to be still oozing blood. His temples and hair are caked with it. There's even a line of blood running down his left cheek. He looks terrible, quite terrible. I wonder if the man knows what it's like to be crucified.

They're stripping his clothes off.

They're also taking off the clothes of the two . . . thieves, I suppose they are. They might be murderers, one can't say. At any rate, they're all having their clothes taken from them. They're naked now.

He's thin, my *God*, he's thin. What brainless sort of faith prescribes starvation for a man?

Excuse my comments, gentlemen. I'm liable to make them without thinking. I have rather definite opinions on this moment and this man.

Jesus is quite emaciated. Muscular though. Quite well built. A little flesh and he'd look . . . almost excellent. Now I can see his face a little better. It's . . . rather handsome. Yes, under ideal circumstances this man *might* be extremely handsome. One might then understand his magnetic control over people, his seeming . . . *aura* of supernatural prescience.

WHAT'S HAPPENING, PROFESSOR?

The soldiers are forcing the three men on their backs. Their arms are being extended along the cross beams. Are they to be lashed or . . .

They *were*—I mean they *are being* . . . Uh! Good God, can you hear the sound of it? Oh my God. Right through their palms! *Sickening* practice. These ancients certainly have their foul ways.

This crucifixion business—a horrible thing. A man can last three or four days if his constitution is strong enough—if he survives the impeded circulation, the headaches, the hunger, the wracking cramps, hemorrhage, syncope of the heart. Either hunger or thirst will get them, probably thirst.

I hope to heaven they don't practice crurifragium, that brutal beating to death with mallets. History says nothing of it in this case but how can anyone know? Except—the idea occurs—except *me*.

WHAT'S HAPPENING?

They're being raised. The soldiers are lifting them with the cross beams. The thieves are jumping up in order to avoid torn palms. They're roaring with anger and pain.

He can't get up. They're—oh God!—they're *pulling* him up by his nailed palms! His face has gone *white*. But he doesn't cry out. His lips are pressed together, they're drained of color. He refuses to cry out. The man's a *fanatic*.

IS THE PLACE CROWDED, PROFESSOR?

No, no, there's no one around. The soldiers are keeping people away. There are a few people but none closer than thirty yards. A few men. And, yes, some women. Three I see together. They could possibly be the three mentioned by Matthew and Mark.

But no one else. I see no man who could be John. No woman who could be the mother of Jesus. And surely I'd recognize Mary of Magdalene. No one but those three women. No one seems to care, that is. The rest, apparently, are here for the . . . the show. Good God how this scene has been garbled and obscured by pious gilding. I can—I can hardly express how *dreary* it all is, how common and ordinary. Not that killing a man this way is ordinary but . . . well, where are the portents, the signs, the miracles?

Biblical drivel.

WHAT'S HAPPENING, JAIRUS?

Well, he's been put up. The cross is, of course, not at all as pictured in religious rite. It's really a low wooden structure resembling a letter T. The stem was already in the ground as I've said and the cross beam was put on top of it and nailed and lashed. The feet of the three men are only inches from the ground. That serves the purpose as well as if it were many feet.

And, speaking of feet, the feet of the three men were lashed, not nailed to the stake. And between their legs is a-a spar, a peg. It supports their bodies. I'd rather expected one under their feet too. Apparently I'm wrong on that count.

It is—*bizarre* though, how people in our time can believe a man weighing—oh, it must be at least one-hundred seventy pounds—could *hang* from a cross merely by nails through palms and feet. They attribute to the human flesh far more durability than it possesses.

Now the soldiers are . . .

WHAT ABOUT THE TITULAR INSCRIPTION, PROFESSOR?

Oh, yes, yes. Well, they *are* in three languages, it appears. There's Greek. There's Hebrew and Latin. Let me see . . . uh . . . *Jesus of . . . Nazareth*—yes—*Jesus of Nazareth. The . . . King . . . King of the Jews.* That's the complete inscription. Have you got that? *Jesus of Nazareth. The King of the Jews.* Apparently John had some factual information about the crucifixion anyway. Even if he isn't here as he claimed.

Ah, yes. The soldiers are holding a drink up to Jesus. I assume it's the soporific intended to induce stupefac-

tion that the Jerusalem women are reputed to have prepared for all such condemned criminals.

Ah. He refuses it. He turns his head to the side. The
soldier is angry. He draws back as if he means to strike
Jesus. But he changes his mind.

The other two men are drinking the wine and myrrh
the soldiers hold to their lips. They're smacking their
lips. One of them says something. I didn't hear all of it.
I heard the word *good* though. They're both smacking
their lips.

One of them, apparently, is asking for the drink Jesus
refused. He doesn't get it. He turns and jeers at Jesus for
not drinking it. He speaks so fast I can't catch his words.
I think he must be half drunk with terror anyway. Soon
he'll be insensible from the drink though. That will be his
release. Jesus chooses to have no release.

That's his privilege as self-appointed martyr.

YOU WERE SAYING BEFORE ABOUT THE
SOLDIERS, PROFESSOR?

The soldiers? Oh—oh *yes.* They're casting lots for the
clothes. I imagine I don't have to tell you that there's no
robe I can see that has no seam. They're all three very
ordinary robes with very visible seams.

Well, that seems to complete the basic details. The three are up. I'll study Jesus now a little. May I move closer?

IF YOU WISH. BUT BE ABSOLUTELY CERTAIN YOU REMAIN WITHIN THE ENERGY SCREEN.

I'll be careful. I'm moving. I'm about six yards away now. Five—three—t . . . this will do. I don't think I should . . . I don't think I'd better get any closer.

IS EVERYTHING ALL RIGHT?

Quite—quite all right, I-uh-*am* a little nervous, that's all. After all, this *is* Jesus. I almost feel as if he can—well, that's absurd. How powerful a hold superstition holds on the mind.

Yes, he's quite young. In his thirties, I'd judge. As I said, in good health and groomed, he might be a stunning figure. He might even understandably be taken for some sort of messianic deliverer.

His skin is clear. Dirty, of course, but . . . clear. His mouth is rather wide, full lipped. A strong line. His nose isn't hooked. It looks almost—oh, I don't know—almost Grecian, you might say. He *is* quite handsome. Yes. He's quite a handsome man.

The eyes are . . .

PROFESSOR?

Well, at least our theories are vindicated that later description of the crucifixion is almost primarily based on prophecy. It's obvious that very little in the Bible transcription of the scene is factual. There is no John, no mother of Jesus, no Mary of Magdalene, no others supposed to be here. I've heard no words from Jesus. No one has jeered at him except that thief and that was only because the thief was angry he didn't get the second drink of drugged wine. And there are no signs.

No, I think we can safely say that the later chroniclers, intent on substantiating the old Psalms auguries, put together the account of the crucifixion with Old Testament in lap. These Psalms, the 22nd, 31st, 38th and 69th to the fore, plus Christian imagination—made the crucifixion something—*quite* different from what it actually was. From what it *is* as I stand here.

I . . . *oh*

. . . .

WHAT IS IT, PROFESSOR?

He just . . . *spoke.*

He spoke. He said—Eloi. He said *God* in his own

language. His face is white and drawn. The lines of *pain* on it . . .

His face—it's so . . . so *gentle*. Even now in this moment of terrible pain, he . . .

Undoubtedly auto-suggested hypnosis, easily effected due to his exhaustion and emotional fervor. I'm sure the poor dev—man must feel some sort of . . . violent ecstasy of pain. Maybe he doesn't even feel pain at all. Perhaps his heightened body functioning, his exacerbated adrenaline flow—prevent feeling. It's perfectly feasible. His eyes are . . . his—his eyes are . . .

ARE THERE ANY SIGNS OF NATURAL DISORDER, PROFESSOR JAIRUS?

I assume you—refer to the earthquake recorded or the dark skies or the tombs rent open or a half dozen other things spoken about in the Bible and other sources.

No, I'm afraid not.

No dark skies. The sun is still very bright and very hot. The ground is as steady as a rock. The records *err* slightly. Obviously the authors of the records weren't satisfied with this and decided to add religious significance to an otherwise unreligious moment. Hand of God and all that rot.

It makes me furious, really. Isn't the moment enough in itself? Isn't it terrible and violent enough for . . . oh, the damnable pedantry of—!

. . . .

PROFESSOR, ARE YOU ALL RIGHT?

What?

ARE YOU ALL RIGHT? ARE YOU FEELING ILL?

I'm . . . quite well. Thank you.

WHAT'S HAPPENING?

. . . .

PROFESSOR?

Those eyes. Those *eyes*. My God, they're so—they're so *hurt!* Like a father who's been beaten by his own children. Yet who still loves his children. Who's been set upon by loved ones and *stripped* and *beaten* and *nailed* and *humiliated!* Is there no—

PROFESSOR.

I'm—I'm—I'm all right. I'm quite—quite all right.

It's just that . . . it *is* upsetting. This man has done nothing and—oh, my God, there's a *fly* on his lips! *Get off!*

. . . .

WHAT'S HAPPENING, PROFESSOR JAIRUS? ARE YOU—

They're giving him a drink. He must be horribly thirsty. The sun is so hot. I'm thirsty myself.

A soldier just dipped a sponge into a pail of *posca*, the soldiers' drink of vinegar and water. Now he's put the sponge on a broken reed which was lying on the ground. He touches the sponge to the mouth of Jesus.

He . . . sucks the sponge. His lips tremble. It must taste horrible—*bitter* and *warm*. God, why don't they give him a real drink—some cool water? Have they no pity for the—

PROFESSOR, YOU'D BETTER GET READY TO COME BACK NOW. YOU'VE BEEN GONE ALMOST FORTY MINUTES ALREADY. YOU'VE DONE WHAT'S TO BE DONE.

No, don't take me back yet—not just yet. A little while. Just a little while. I'll be all right. I swear I'll be all right. J-just let me—stay here with him. Don't take me, not now. *Please.*

PROFESSOR JAIRUS.

His eyes, his eyes—*his eyes!* Oh my God in heaven, they're looking at me! He *sees* me! I'm sure of it! He *sees* me!

WE'RE BRINGING YOU BACK.

No, not yet. I'm—I must . . . I . . .

DON'T GET OUT OF THE SCREEN.

Out of the screen? Yes, maybe I can—I could . . .

YOU'RE COMING BACK.

No! No, I'll break the screen if you try to bring me back! I'll—I'll go *through* it! I swear I will—don't touch me!

PROFESSOR, STOP IT!

I've got to stop them! I've got to *stop* them! I'm here, I can save him! I *can!* Why can't I take him into the screen with me and take him away?

JAIRUS, USE YOUR HEAD!

Why not, damn it, why *not!* I'm not going to stand here and let them destroy him! He's too good, too gentle. I can save him—I *can!*

JAIRUS, YOU'VE DONE YOUR JOB! NOW LET HIM DO *HIS!*

No!

LOCK THE SCREEN.

What! What are you doing?

WE'LL HAVE TO CHANCE BRINGING HIM BACK IN THE FEW SECONDS THE SCREEN LOCK WILL HOLD.

Let me out! God help me, let me free! Stop it, you don't know what you're doing!

QUICKLY!

No! Stop—*stop!* Don't take me! *Don't!* LOOK OUT!

They dragged him, frenzied and kicking from the platform. They carried him into the office and put him down on a cot and Doctor Randall drove a syringe into his arm.

In a half hour Professor Jairus was quiet enough to swallow a glass of brandy. He sat in a big leather chair, staring straight ahead, his eyes lifeless. His mind had not returned with his body—it was still back on a lonely hill beyond Jerusalem.

There were things he could have told them; word pictures to bolster history. He could have described the clothes worn on Golgotha, the words spoken there, the moment in its bleak and brutal entirety—all this he could have told them. Told them especially that, in bringing him back so quickly, they had caused the phenomena which the Bible recorded as a quaking of earth and a renting of rocks.

None of these things did he tell them.

He told them he wanted to go home.

He put on his coat and hat and overshoes and walked into the gray murk of afternoon. His rubber covered shoes crunched in the hard packed snow, his eyes stared into the curtain of soft-falling snow.

The other things are not important, he was thinking. True or untrue they didn't matter. The water into wine, the lepers cleansed, the sick healed, the walking on water, the return from the grave—none of them mattered. Men who sought for hope in physical miracles only were childish dreamers who could never save the world.

A man had given up his life for the things he believed in. *That was miracle enough for anyone.*

It was Christmas Eve and it was a lovely time to find a faith.

WHEN DAY IS DUN

Now bray goodnight to Earth
For day is dun and man's estate
Is cast into the vault of time
Tuck in the graveclothes of forever
Snuff the candle of attempt
And let fall across our eyes
That secret shroud of fusion
With dark mystery.

He sat upon a rock and wrote his text on wood, using as pen a charcoaled finger. It is just, he mused, that the concluding theme should be set down with this digit in limbo, this beggarly palpus which once pointed at earth and sky to arrogate—I am your master, earth, your master, sky—and now lies grilled and temperate among the rubbish of our being.

I sit at Earth's wake and shed no tear.

Now he raised funereal eyes to float across the plain a glacial contemplation. Between his fingers rolled the sooty stylus and breath showed nasal evidence of his disgust. Now here am I, he brooded, perched upon a tepid boulder and inspecting that momentous joke which man has finally played upon himself.

He smote his brow and "*Ah!*" he cried, spiritually swept overboard. His great despairing head flopped forward on his chest and quavering moans beset his form. Birthright disemboweled, he sorrowed, golden chance arust, man has found the way—but to extinction.

Then he straightened up to make his back a ramrod of defiance. I shall not be a cur bowwowing, he avowed. This mortuary moment shall not have the best of me. Yea, though death bestride me and plucks with spectral fingers at my sores I shall not cry for less; I am inviolate.

The tatters quivered royally upon his shoulders. He bent to write again:

> *Now let me relish death*
> *As Earth gloats o'er her own demise*
> *With eyes of shimmering slag.*

One leaden edge of tongue peeped out through barricades of lip. Now he was hot.

> *Birds crow a serenade to man*
> *Incinerated he*
> *Prostrate sauteed skeleton*
> *For all the gods to see*
> *Birds peck a saucy tune with bristly nibs*
> *Upon the xylophone of man's forgotten ribs.*

"Capital! *Capital!*" he cried, stamping one unbooted foot upon the ashy soil. In the excitement of the phrase, he dropped his pen and stopped to pluck it up. Here, deposed antennae, he grimaced the thought, and then he wrote again.

Odd it was, he scrolled, *that man throughout his ill-tuned history never ceased to plot man's own destruction.*

Chorus: *More than fantastic*
This alien two
Lived together
And never knew.

He paused. How to continue, he wondered, how go on with this concluding ledger of man's account? It demanded bite, a trenchant instantaneity and yet deceptive calm like forty fathom sea when gales are shrieking overhead. As there, so here, he thought, I must suggest the titanic with polished and well-mannered couplets. As for instance:

Tell me here
What difference there
To burn in bias
Or burn in fires.

I have no audience nor hope of one yet I go on composing till what needs be said is said. And then I go—my own way.

He reached into his pocket for the twenty-seventh time and drawing out the pistol, rolled its chamber with reflective finger. One bullet there he knew, his key to final rest. He gazed into the barrel's dark eye and did not quail. Yes, when it ends, he thought, when I have savored to the dregs this dark wine of most utter ruination, I shall press this to my head and blow away the last of man's complaints.

But now, he thought, back to my work. I have not done with mankind yet. A few words still remain, several discourteous racks of poesy. Shall I dispose so soon of what men always wanted most—the last word?

He flourished stylus, wrote:

> *Be this the final entry*
> *In mankind's book of psalms*
> *He knit his shroud with atoms*
> *And dug his grave with bombs.*

No. No, that did not catch the temper. He scratched it out. Let me see, he tapped a nail upon eroded teeth. What can I say? Ah!

> *Man the better*
> *Man the higher*

Man the pumps
The world's on fire.

But is this all quite fair, he mused amid chuckling, that I, as sole survivor, make such light of this unnatural tragedy which is the fall of man. Should I not instead sing out of mountainous regrets and summon tidal panegyrics which would wash away all bitterness with one great, cleansing surge. Should I not?

Man, man, he brooded, what have you done with your so excellent a world? Was it so small that you should scorn it, so drafty you should heat it to an incandescence, so unsightly you should rearrange its mountains and its seas?

"Ah," he said, "oh . . . *ah!*"

His hands fell limp. A tear, two tears ran down his beak-shape nose to quiver on the tip, then fall upon the ground. And hiss.

What portent this, his mind groaned on, that I should be the last of Man's embittered tribe. The very last! Portent this, vast moment this—to be alone in all the world!

It is too much, he cried aloud within his head. I reel

at the significance. He fingered the gun. How can I bear to hold this crushing weight upon my shoulders? Are my words appropriate, my sentiments all fit for this immensity of meaning?

He blinked, released the pistol. He was insulted by the question. What, *I* not up to it; what, *my* words inappropriate? He straightened up and bristled at the ash-envapored sky.

It is *fitting*, he declared, that these last measures be composed by a man alone. For shall a pack of masons clamor round the stone, entangling arms in clumsy eagerness to chisel out man's epitaph? And shall a host of scriveners haggle endlessly on man's obituary, muttering and wrangling like a coachless football team in huddle?

No this is best—one man to suffer beautiful agonies, one voice to speak the final words, then dot the i's and cross the t's and so farewell to Man's domain—ending, if not sustaining, in gentle poetry.

And *I* that man, *I* that voice! Blessed with this final opportunity, my words alone without a million others to dilute them, my phrases only to ring out through all eternity, uncontradicted.

He sighed, he wrote again.

It took this to make me individual
The killing of all men
Yea . . .

His head jerked up, alarmed, as, from far across the rubbled plain there came a sound.

"Eh?" he muttered. "What be that?"

He blinked, re-focused blood-streaked eyes, shook his head, squinted. And then his lower jaw slipped down and down until his mouth became a yawning cave.

A man was hobbling across the plain, waving a crooked arm at him. He watched the ashes rise in clouds of powder around the limping man and, in his mind, a great numbness struck.

A fellow creature! A comrade, another voice to hear, another . . .

The man stumbled up.

"Friend!" cried the man from out his startled face.

And abruptly, hearing this human voice usurp the mountainous, brooding silence, something suddenly snapped within the poet's brain.

"I shall not be robbed!" he cried. And he shot the man neatly between the eyes. Then he stepped across the peaceful body and went over to another rock of fused sidewalk.

He sat, shook back his sleeve. And, just before he bent to work again, he spun the empty chambers in his hand.

Ah, well, he sighed, for this moment, to have this glorious, shining doom alone—it was worth it.

Sonnet to a Parboiled Planet, he began . . .

THE SPLENDID SOURCE

Then spare me your slanders, and read this rather at night than in the daytime, and give it not to young maidens, if there be any . . . But I fear nothing for this book, since it is extracted from a high and splendid source, from which all that has issued has had a great success.

—Balzac: *Contes Drolatiques*, Prologue

It was the one Uncle Lyman told in the summer house that did it. Talbert was just coming up the path when he heard the punch line: " 'My God!' cried the actress, 'I thought you said *sarsaparilla!* ' "

Guffaws exploded in the little house. Talbert stood motionless, looking through the rose trellis at the laughing guests. Inside his contour sandals his toes flexed ruminatively. He thought.

Later he took a walk around Lake Bean and watched the crystal surf fold over and observed the gliding swans and stared at the goldfish and thought.

"I've been thinking," he said that night.

"No," said Uncle Lyman, haplessly. He did not commit himself further. He waited for the blow.

Which fell.

"Dirty jokes," said Talbert Bean III.

"I beg your pardon?" said Uncle Lyman.

"Endless tides of them covering the nation."

"I fail," said Uncle Lyman, "to grasp the point." Apprehension gripped his voice.

"I find the subject fraught with witchery," said Talbert.

"With—?"

"Consider," said Talbert. "Every day, all through our land, men tell off-color jokes; in bars and at ball games;

in theater lobbies and at places of business; on street corners and in locker rooms. At home and away, a veritable deluge of jokes."

Talbert paused meaningfully,

"*Who makes them up?*" he asked.

Uncle Lyman stared at his nephew with the look of a fisherman who has just hooked a sea serpent—half awe, half revulsion.

"I'm afraid—" he began.

"I want to know the source of these jokes," said Talbert. "Their genesis; their fountainhead."

"*Why?*" asked Uncle Lyman. Weakly.

"Because it is relevant," said Talbert. "Because these jokes are a part of a culture heretofore unplumbed. Because they are an anomaly; a phenomenon ubiquitous yet unknown."

Uncle Lyman did not speak. His pallid hands curled limply on his half-read *Wall Street Journal.* Behind the polished octagons of his glasses his eyes were suspended berries.

At last he sighed.

"And what part," he inquired sadly, "am I to play in this quest?"

"We must begin," said Talbert, "with the joke you

told in the summer house this afternoon. Where did you hear it?"

"Kulpritt," Uncle Lyman said. Andrew Kulpritt was one of the battery of lawyers employed by Bean Enterprises.

"Capital," said Talbert. "Call him up and ask him where *he* heard it."

Uncle Lyman drew the silver watch from his pocket.

"It's nearly midnight, Talbert," he announced.

Talbert waved away chronology.

"*Now*," he said. "This is important."

Uncle Lyman examined his nephew a moment longer. Then, with a capitulating sigh, he reached for one of Bean Mansion's thirty-five telephones.

Talbert stood toe-flexed on a bearskin rug while Uncle Lyman dialed, waited and spoke.

"Kulpritt?" said Uncle Lyman. "Lyman Bean. Sorry to wake you but Talbert wants to know where you heard the joke about the actress who thought the director said sarsaparilla."

Uncle Lyman listened. "I said—" he began again.

A minute later he cradled the receiver heavily.

"Prentiss," he said.

"Call him up," said Talbert.

"*Talbert*," Uncle Lyman asked.

"Now," said Talbert.

A long breath exuded between Uncle Lyman's lips. Carefully, he folded his *Wall Street Journal.* He reached across the mahogany table and tamped out his ten-inch cigar. Sliding a weary hand beneath his smoking jacket, he withdrew his tooled leather address book.

Prentiss heard it from George Sharper, CPA Sharper heard it from Abner Ackerman, MD. Ackerman heard it from William Cozener, Prune Products. Cozener heard it from Rod Tassell, Mgr., Cyprian Club. Tassell heard it from O. Winterbottom. Winterbottom heard it from H. Alberts. Alberts heard it from D. Silver, Silver from B. Phryne, Phryne from E. Kennelly.

By an odd twist Kennelly said he heard it from Uncle Lyman.

"There is complicity here," said Talbert. "These jokes are not self-generative."

It was four a.m. Uncle Lyman slumped, inert and dead-eyed, on his chair.

"There has to be a source," said Talbert.

Uncle Lyman remained motionless.

"You're not interested," said Talbert, incredulously.

Uncle Lyman made a noise.

"I don't understand," said Talbert. "Here is a situation

pregnant with divers fascinations. Is there a man or woman who has never heard an off-color joke? I say not. Yet, is there a man or woman who knows where these jokes come from? Again I say not."

Talbert strode forcefully to his place of musing at the twelve-foot fireplace. He poised there, staring in.

"I may be a millionaire," he said, "but I am sensitive." He turned. "And this phenomenon excites me."

Uncle Lyman attempted to sleep while retaining the face of a man awake.

"I have always had more money than I needed," said Talbert. "Capital investment was unnecessary. Thus I turned to investing the other asset my father left—my brain."

Uncle Lyman stirred; a thought shook loose.

"What ever happened," he asked, "to that society of yours, the S.P.C.S.P.C.A.?"

"The Society for the Prevention of Cruelty to the Society for the Prevention of Cruelty to Animals? The past."

"What about that sociological treatise you were writing . . ."

"*Slums: A Positive View?*" Talbert brushed it aside. "Inconsequence."

"Isn't there anything left of your political party, the Pro-antidisestablishmentarianists?"

"Not a shred. Scuttled by reactionaries from within."

"What about Bimetallism?"

Talbert smiled ruefully. "Passé, dear Uncle. I had been reading too many Victorian novels."

"Speaking of novels, what about your literary criticisms? *The Use of the Semicolon in Jane Austen*? *Horatio Alger: The Misunderstood Satirist*? To say nothing of *Was Queen Elizabeth Shakespeare*?"

"*Was Shakespeare Queen Elizabeth*," corrected Talbert. "No, Uncle, nothing doing with them. They had momentary interest, not more . . ."

"I suppose the same holds true for *The Shoe Horn: Pro and Con*, eh? And those scientific articles—*Relativity Re-Examined* and *Is Evolution Enough*?"

"Dead and gone," said Talbert, patiently. "Those projects needed me once. Now I go on to better things."

"Like who writes dirty jokes," said Uncle Lyman.

Talbert nodded.

"Like that," he said.

. . .

When the butler set the breakfast tray on the bed Talbert said, "Redfield, do you know any jokes?"

Redfield looked out impassively through the face an improvident nature had neglected to animate.

"Jokes, sir?" he inquired.

"You know," said Talbert. "Jollities."

Redfield stood by the bed like a corpse whose casket had been upended and removed.

"Well, sir," he said, a full thirty seconds later, "once, when I was a boy I heard one . . ."

"Yes?" said Talbert eagerly.

"I believe it went somewhat as follows," Redfield said. "When—uh—*When* is a portmanteau not a—"

"No, no," said Talbert, shaking his head. "I mean *dirty* jokes."

Redfield's eyebrows soared. The vernacular was like a fish in his face.

"You don't know any?" said a disappointed Talbert.

"Begging your pardon, sir," said Redfield. "If I may make a suggestion. May I say that the chauffeur is more likely to—"

"You know any dirty jokes, Harrison?" Talbert asked through the tube as the Rolls Royce purred along Bean Road toward Highway 27.

Harrison looked blank for a moment. He glanced back at Talbert. Then a grin wrinkled his carnal jowls.

"Well, sir," he began, "there's this guy sittin' by the burlesque runway eatin' an onion, see?"

Talbert unclipped his four-color pencil.

Talbert stood in an elevator rising to the tenth floor of the Gault Building.

The hour ride to New York had been most illuminating. Not only had he transcribed seven of the most horrendously vulgar jokes he had ever heard in his life but had exacted a promise from Harrison to take him to the various establishments where these jokes had been heard.

The hunt was on.

MAX AXE / DETECTIVE AGENCY read the words on the frosty-glassed door. Talbert turned the knob and went in.

Announced by the beautiful receptionist, Talbert was ushered into a sparsely furnished office on whose walls were a hunting license, a machine gun, and framed photographs of the Seagram factory, the St. Valentine's Day Massacre in color and Herbert J. Philbrick who had led three lives.

Mr. Axe shook Talbert's hand.

"What could I do for ya?" he asked.

"First of all," said Talbert, "do you know any dirty jokes?"

Recovering, Mr. Axe told Talbert the one about the monkey and the elephant.

Talbert jotted it down. Then he hired the agency to investigate the men Uncle Lyman had phoned and uncover anything that was meaningful.

After he left the agency, Talbert began making the rounds with Harrison. He heard a joke the first place they went.

"There's this midget in a frankfurter suit, see?" it began.

It was a day of buoyant discovery. Talbert heard the joke about the cross-eyed plumber in the harem, the one about the preacher who won an eel at a raffle, the one about the fighter pilot who went down in flames and the one about the two Girl Scouts who lost their cookies in the laundromat.

Among others.

"I want," said Talbert, "one round-trip airplane ticket to San Francisco and a reservation at the Hotel Millard Fillmore."

"May I ask," asked Uncle Lyman, "why?"

"While making the rounds with Harrison today," explained Talbert, "a salesman of ladies' undergarments told me a veritable cornucopia of off-color jokes exists in the person of Harry Shuler, bellboy at the Millard Fillmore. This salesman said that, during a three-day convention at that hotel, he heard more new jokes from Shuler than he had heard in the first thirty-nine years of his life."

"And you are going to—?" Uncle Lyman began.

"Exactly," said Talbert. "We must follow where the spoor is strongest."

"Talbert," said Uncle Lyman, "why do you *do* these things?"

"I am searching," said Talbert simply.

"For what, dammit!" cried Uncle Lyman.

"For *meaning*," said Talbert.

Uncle Lyman covered his eyes. "You are the image of your mother," he declared.

"Say nothing of her," charged Talbert. "She was the finest woman who ever trod the earth."

"Then how come she got trampled to death at the funeral of Rudolph Valentino?" Uncle Lyman charged back.

"That is a base canard," said Talbert, "and you know it. Mother just happened to be passing the church on her way to bringing food to the Orphans of the Dissolute Seamen—one of her many charities—when she was accidentally caught up in the waves of hysterical women and swept to her awful end."

A pregnant silence bellied the vast room. Talbert stood at a window looking down the hill at Lake Bean which his father had had poured in 1923.

"Think of it," he said after a moment's reflection. "The nation alive with off-color jokes—the *world* alive! And the same jokes, Uncle, *the same jokes*. How? *How?* By what strange means do these jokes o'erleap oceans, span continents? By what incredible machinery are these jokes promulgated over mountain and dale?"

He turned and met Uncle Lyman's mesmeric stare.

"*I mean to know*," he said.

At ten minutes before midnight Talbert boarded the plane for San Francisco and took a seat by the window. Fifteen minutes later the plane roared down the runway and nosed up into the black sky.

Talbert turned to the man beside him.

"Do you know any dirty jokes, sir?" he inquired, pencil poised.

The man stared at him. Talbert gulped.

"Oh, I *am* sorry," he said, "Reverend."

When they reached the room Talbert gave the bellboy a crisp five-dollar bill and asked to hear a joke.

Shuler told him the one about the man sitting by the burlesque runway eating an onion, see? Talbert listened, toes kneading inquisitively in his shoes. The joke concluded, he asked Shuler where this and similar jokes might be overheard. Shuler said at a wharf spot known as Davy Jones' Locker Room.

Early that evening, after drinking with one of the West Coast representatives of Bean Enterprises, Talbert took a taxi to Davy Jones' Locker Room. Entering its dim, smoke-fogged interior, he took a place at the bar, ordered a Screwdriver and began to listen.

Within an hour's time he had written down the joke about the old maid who caught her nose in the bathtub faucet, the one about the three traveling salesmen and the farmer's ambidextrous daughter, the one about the nurse who thought they were Spanish olives and the one about the midget in the frankfurter suit. Talbert wrote this last joke under his original transcription of it, underlining changes in context attributable to regional influence.

At 10:16, a man who had just told Talbert the one about the hillbilly twins and their two-headed sister said that Tony, the bartender, was a virtual faucet of off-color jokes, limericks, anecdotes, epigrams and proverbs.

Talbert went over to the bar and asked Tony for the major source of his lewdiana. After reciting the limerick about the sex of the asteroid vermin, the bartender referred Talbert to a Mr. Frank Bruin, salesman, of Oakland, who happened not to be there that night.

Talbert at once retired to a telephone directory where he discovered five Frank Bruins in Oakland. Entering a booth with a coat pocket sagging change, Talbert began dialing them.

Two of the five Frank Bruins were salesmen. One of them, however, was in Alcatraz at the moment. Talbert traced the remaining Frank Bruin to Hogan's Alleys in Oakland where his wife said that, as usual on Thursday nights, her husband was bowling with the Moonlight Mattress Company All-Stars.

Quitting the bar, Talbert chartered a taxi and started across the bay to Oakland, toes in ferment.

Veni, vidi, vici?

. . .

Bruin was not a needle in a haystack.

The moment Talbert entered Hogan's Alleys his eye was caught by a football huddle of men encircling a portly, rosy-domed speaker. Approaching, Talbert was just in time to hear the punch line followed by an explosion of composite laughter. It was the punch line that intrigued.

" 'My God!' cried the actress," Mr. Bruin had uttered, " 'I thought you said a *banana split!* ' "

This variation much excited Talbert who saw in it a verification of a new element—the interchangeable kicker.

When the group had broken up and drifted, Talbert accosted Mr. Bruin and, introducing himself, asked where Mr. Bruin had heard that joke.

"Why d'ya ask, boy?" asked Mr. Bruin.

"No reason," said the crafty Talbert.

"I don't remember where I heard it, boy," said Mr. Bruin finally. "Excuse me, will ya?"

Talbert trailed after him but received no satisfaction— unless it was in the most definite impression that Bruin was concealing something.

Later, riding back to the Millard Fillmore, Talbert

decided to put an Oakland detective agency on Mr. Bruin's trail to see what could be seen.

When Talbert reached the hotel there was a telegram waiting for him at the desk.

> *Mr. Rodney Tassell received long distance call from Mr. George Bullock, Carthage Hotel, Chi-cago. Was told joke about midget in salami suit. Meaningful?—Axe.*

Talbert's eyes ignited.

"Tally," he murmured, "*ho.*"

An hour later he had checked out of the Millard Fillmore, taxied to the airport and caught a plane for Chicago.

Twenty minutes after he had left the hotel, a man in a dark pin-stripe approached the desk clerk and asked for the room number of Talbert Bean III. When informed of Talbert's departure the man grew steely-eyed and immediately retired to a telephone booth. He emerged ashen.

"I'm sorry," said the desk clerk, "Mr. Bullock checked out this morning."

"Oh." Talbert's shoulders sagged. All night on the plane he had been checking over his notes, hoping to discern a pattern to the jokes which would emcompass type, area of genesis and periodicity. He was weary with fruitless concentration. Now this.

"And he left no forwarding address?" he asked.

"Only Chicago, sir," said the clerk.

"I see."

Following a bath and luncheon in his room, a slightly refreshed Talbert settled down with the telephone and the directory. There were forty-seven George Bullocks in Chicago. Talbert checked them off as he phoned.

At three o'clock he slumped over the receiver in a dead slumber. At 4:21, he regained consciousness and completed the remaining eleven calls. The Mr. Bullock in question was not at home, said his housekeeper, but was expected in that evening.

"Thank you kindly," said a bleary-eyed Talbert and, hanging up, thereupon collapsed on the bed—only to awake a few minutes past seven and dress quickly. Descending to the street, he gulped down a sandwich and a glass of milk, then hailed a cab and made the hour ride to the home of George Bullock.

The man himself answered the bell.

"Yes?" he asked.

Talbert introduced himself and said he had come to the Hotel Carthage early that afternoon to see him.

"Why?" asked Mr. Bullock.

"So you could tell me where you heard that joke about the midget in the salami suit," said Talbert.

"*Sir?*"

"I said—"

"I heard what you said, sir," said Mr. Bullock, "though I cannot say that your remark makes any noticeable sense."

"I believe, sir," challenged Talbert, "that you are hiding behind fustian."

"Behind fustian, sir?" retorted Bullock. "I'm afraid—"

"The game is up, sir!" declared Talbert in a ringing voice. "Why don't you admit it and tell me where you got that joke from?"

"I have not the remotest conception of what you're talking about, sir!" snapped Bullock, his words belied by the pallor of his face.

Talbert flashed a Mona Lisa smile.

"Indeed?" he said.

And, turning lightly on his heel, he left Bullock trembling in the doorway. As he settled back against the taxi-cab seat again, he saw Bullock still standing there staring at him. Then Bullock whirled and was gone.

"Hotel Carthage," said Talbert, satisfied with his bluff.

Riding back, he thought of Bullock's agitation and a thin smile tipped up the corners of his mouth. No doubt about it. The prey was being run to earth. Now if his surmise was valid there would likely be—

A lean man in a raincoat and a derby was sitting on the bed when Talbert entered his room. The man's mustache, like a muddy toothbrush, twitched.

"Talbert Bean?" he asked.

Talbert bowed.

"The same," he said.

The man, a Colonel Bishop, retired, looked at Talbert with metal-blue eyes.

"What is your game, sir?" he asked tautly.

"I don't understand," toyed Talbert.

"I think you do," said the Colonel, "and you are to come with me."

"Oh?" said Talbert.

To find himself looking down the barrel of a .45-caliber Webley-Fosbery.

"Shall we?" said the Colonel.

"But of course," said Talbert coolly. "I have not come all this way to resist now."

The ride in the private plane was a long one. The windows were blacked out and Talbert hadn't the faintest idea in which direction they were flying. Neither the pilot nor the Colonel spoke, and Talbert's attempts at conversation were discouraged by a chilly silence. The Colonel's pistol, still leveled at Talbert's chest, never wavered, but it did not bother Talbert. He was exultant. All he could think was that his search was ending; he was, at last, approaching the headwaters of the dirty joke. After a time, his head nodded and he dozed—to dream of midgets in frankfurter suits and actresses who seemed obsessed by sarsaparilla or banana splits or sometimes both. How long he slept, and what boundaries he may have crossed, Talbert never knew. He was awakened by a swift loss of altitude and the steely voice of Colonel Bishop: "We are landing, Mr. Bean." The Colonel's grip tightened on the pistol.

Talbert offered no resistance when his eyes were blindfolded. Feeling the Webley-Fosbery in the small of his back, he stumbled out of the plane and crunched over the ground of a well-kept airstrip. There was a nip in the air and he felt a bit lightheaded. Talbert suspected they had landed in a mountainous region; but what mountains, and on what continent, he could not guess. His ears and nose conveyed nothing of help to his churning mind.

He was shoved—none too gently—into an automobile, and then driven swiftly along what felt like a dirt road. The tires crackled over pebbles and twigs.

Suddenly the blindfold was removed. Talbert blinked and looked out the windows. It was a black and cloudy night; he could see nothing but the limited vista afforded by the headlights.

"You are well isolated," he said, appreciatively. Colonel Bishop remained tight-lipped and vigilant.

After a fifteen-minute ride along the dark road, the car pulled up in front of a tall, unlighted house. As the motor was cut Talbert could hear the pulsing rasp of crickets all around.

"Well," he said.

"Emerge," suggested Colonel Bishop.

"Of course." Talbert bent out of the car and was escorted up the wide porch steps by the Colonel. Behind, the car pulled away into the night.

Inside the house, chimes bonged hollowly as the Colonel pushed a button. They waited in the darkness and, in a few moments, approaching footsteps sounded.

A tiny aperture opened in the heavy door, disclosing a single bespectacled eye. The eye blinked once and, with a faint accent Talbert could not recognize, whispered furtively, "Why did the widow wear black garters?"

"In remembrance," said Colonel Bishop with great gravity, "of those who passed beyond."

The door opened.

The owner of the eye was tall, gaunt, of indeterminable age and nationality, his hair a dark mass wisped with gray. His face was all angles and facets, his eyes piercing behind large, horn-rimmed glasses. He wore flannel trousers and a checked jacket.

"This is the Dean," said Colonel Bishop.

"How do you do," said Talbert.

"Come *in*, come *in*," the Dean invited, extending his large hand to Talbert. "Welcome, Mr. Bean." He shafted a scolding look at Bishop's pistol. "Now, Colonel," he said, "indulging in melodramatics again? Put it away, dear fellow, put it away."

"We can't be too careful," grumped the Colonel.

Talbert stood in the spacious grace of the entry hall

looking around. His gaze settled, presently, on the cryptic smile of the Dean, who said: "So. You have found us out, sir."

Talbert's toes whipped like pennants in a gale.

He covered his excitement with, "Have I?"

"Yes," said the Dean. "You have. And a masterful display of investigative intuition it was."

Talbert looked around.

"So," he said, voice bated. "It is *here*."

"Yes," said the Dean. "Would you like to see it?"

"*More than anything in the world*," said Talbert fervently.

"Come then," said the Dean.

"Is this wise?" the Colonel warned.

"Come," repeated the Dean.

The three men started down the hallway. For a moment, a shade of premonition darkened Talbert's mind. It was being made so easy. Was it a trap? In a second the thought had slipped away, washed off by a current of excited curiosity.

They started up a winding marble staircase.

"How did you suspect?" the Dean inquired. "That is to say—what prompted you to probe the matter?"

"I just *thought*," said Talbert meaningfully. "Here are

all these jokes yet no one seems to know where they come from. Or *care*."

"Yes," observed the Dean, "we count upon that disinterest. What man in ten million ever asks, where did you hear that joke? Absorbed in memorizing the joke for future use, he gives no thought to its source. This, of course, is our protection."

The Dean smiled at Talbert. "But not," he amended, "from men such as you."

Talbert's flush went unnoticed.

They reached the landing and began walking along a wide corridor lit on each side by the illumination of candelabra. There was no more talk. At the end of the corridor they turned right and stopped in front of massive, iron-hinged doors.

"Is this wise?" the Colonel asked again.

"Too late to stop now," said the Dean and Talbert felt a shiver flutter down his spine. What if it *was* a trap? He swallowed, then squared his shoulders. The Dean had said it. It was too late to stop now.

The great doors tracked open.

"*Et voilà*—," said the Dean.

. . .

The hallway was an avenue. Thick wall-to-wall carpeting sponged beneath Talbert's feet as he walked between the Colonel and the Dean. At periodic intervals along the ceiling hung music-emitting speakers; Talbert recognized the *Gaieté Parisienne.* His gaze moved to a petitpointed tapestry on which Dionysian acts ensued above the stitched motto, "Happy Is the Man Who Is Making Something."

"Incredible," he murmured. "Here; in this house."

"Exactly," said the Dean.

Talbert shook his head wonderingly.

"To think," he said.

The Dean paused before a glass wall and, braking, Talbert peered into an office. Among its rich appointments strode a young man in a striped silk weskit with brass buttons, gesturing meaningfully with a long cigar while, crosslegged on a leather couch, sat a happily sweatered blonde of rich dimensions.

The man stopped briefly and waved to the Dean, smiled, then returned to his spirited dictating.

"One of our best," the Dean said.

"But," stammered Talbert, "I thought that man was on the staff of—"

"He is," said the Dean. "And, in his spare time, he is also one of us."

Talbert followed on excitement-numbed legs.

"But I had no idea," he said. "I presumed the organization to be composed of men like Bruin and Bullock."

"They are merely our means of promulgation," explained the Dean. "Our word-of-mouthers, you might say. Our *creators* come from more exalted ranks—executives, statesmen, the better professional comics, editors, novelists—"

The Dean broke off as the door to one of the other offices opened and a barrelly, bearded man in hunting clothes emerged. He shouldered past them, muttering true things to himself.

"Off again?" the Dean asked pleasantly. The big man grunted. It was a true grunt. He clumped off, lonely for a veldt.

"*Unbelievable*," said Talbert. "Such men as these?"

"Exactly," said the Dean.

They strolled on past the rows of busy offices, Talbert tourist-eyed, the Dean smiling his mandarin smile, the Colonel working his lips as if anticipating the kiss of a toad.

"But where did it all begin?" a dazed Talbert asked.

"That is history's secret," rejoined the Dean, "veiled behind time's opacity. Our venture does have its honored past, however. Great men have graced its cause— Ben Franklin, Mark Twain, Dickens, Swinburne, Rabelais, Balzac; oh, the honor roll is long. Shakespeare, of course, and his friend Ben Jonson. Still farther back, Chaucer, Boccaccio. Further yet, Horace and Seneca, Demosthenes and Plautus. Aristophanes, Apuleius. Yea, in the palaces of Tutankhaumen was our work done; in the black temples of Ahriman, the pleasure dome of Kubla Khan. Where did it begin? Who knows? Scraped on rock, in many a primordial cave, are certain drawings. And there are those among us who believe that these were left by the earliest members of the Brotherhood. But this, of course, is only legend. . . ."

Now they had reached the end of the hallway and were starting down a cushioned ramp.

"There must be vast sums of money involved in this," said Talbert.

"*Heaven forfend*," declared the Dean, stopping short. "Do not confuse our work with alley vending. Our workers contribute freely of their time and skill, caring for naught save the Cause."

"Forgive me," Talbert said. Then, rallying, he asked, "What Cause?"

The Dean's gaze fused on inward things. He ambled on slowly, arms behind his back.

"The Cause of Love," he said, "as opposed to Hate. Of Nature, as opposed to the Unnatural. Of Humanity, as opposed to Inhumanity. Of Freedom, as opposed to Constraint. Of Health, as opposed to Disease. Yes, Mr. Bean, disease. The disease called bigotry; the frighteningly communicable disease that taints all it touches; turns warmth to chill and joy to guilt and good to bad. What Cause?" He stopped dramatically. "The Cause of Life, Mr. Bean—as opposed to Death!"

The Dean lifted a challenging finger. "We see ourselves," he said, "as an army of dedicated warriors marching on the strongholds of prudery. Knights Templar with a just and joyous mission."

"Amen to that," a fervent Talbert said.

They entered a large, cubicle-bordered room. Talbert saw men; some typing, some writing, some staring, some on telephones, talking in a multitude of tongues. Their expressions were, as one, intently aloft. At the far end of the room, expression unseen, a man stabbed plugs into a many-eyed switchboard.

"Our Apprentice Room," said the Dean, "wherein we groom our future . . ."

His voice died off as a young man exited one of the cubicles and approached them, paper in hand, a smile tremulous on his lips.

"Oliver," said the Dean, nodding once.

"I've done a joke, sir," said Oliver. "May I—?"

"But of course," said the Dean.

Oliver cleared viscid anxiety from his throat, then told a joke about a little boy and girl watching a doubles match on the nudist colony tennis court. The Dean smiled, nodding. Oliver looked up, pained.

"No?" he said.

"It is not without merit," encouraged the Dean, "but, as it now stands, you see, it smacks rather too reminiscently of the duchess-butler effect, *Wife of Bath* category. Not to mention the justifiably popular double reverse bishop-barmaid gambit."

"Oh, sir," grieved Oliver, "I'll never prevail."

"Nonsense," said the Dean, adding kindly, "*son*. These shorter jokes are, by all odds, the most difficult to master. They must be cogent, precise; must say something of pith and moment."

"Yes, sir," murmured Oliver.

"Check with Wojciechowski and Sforzini," said the Dean. "Also Ahmed El-Hakim. They'll brief you on use of the Master Index. Eh?" He patted Oliver's back.

"Yes, sir." Oliver managed a smile and returned to his cubicle. The Dean sighed.

"A somber business," he declared. "He'll never be Class-A. He really shouldn't be in the composing end of it at all but—" He gestured meaningfully, "—there is sentiment involved."

"Oh?" said Talbert.

"Yes," said the Dean. "It was his great grandfather who, on June 23, 1848, wrote the first Traveling Salesman joke, American strain."

The Dean and the Colonel lowered their heads a moment in reverent commemoration. Talbert did the same.

"And so we have it," said the Dean. They were back downstairs, sitting in the great living room, sherry having been served.

"Perhaps you wish to know more," said the Dean.

"Only one thing," said Talbert.

"And that is, sir?"

"Why have you shown it to me?"

"Yes," said the Colonel, fingering at his armpit holster, "why indeed?"

The Dean looked at Talbert carefully as if balancing his reply.

"You haven't guessed?" he said, at last. "No, I can see you haven't. Mr. Bean . . . you are not unknown to us. Who has not heard of your work, your unflagging devotion to sometimes obscure but always worthy causes? What man can help but admire your selflessness, your dedication, your proud defiance of convention and prejudice?" The Dean paused and leaned forward.

"Mr. Bean," he said softly. "Talbert—may I call you that?—*we want you on our team.*"

Talbert gaped. His hands began to tremble. The Colonel, relieved, grunted and sank back into his chair.

No reply came from the flustered Talbert, so the Dean continued, "Think it over. Consider the merits of our work. With all due modesty, I think I may say that here is your opportunity to ally yourself with the greatest cause of your life."

"I'm speechless," said Talbert. "I hardly—that is— how can I . . ."

But, already, the light of consecration was stealing into his eyes.

LEMMINGS

"Where do they all come from?" Reordon asked.

"Everywhere," said Carmack.

They were standing on the coast highway. As far as they could see there was nothing but cars. Thousands of cars were jammed bumper to bumper and pressed side to side. The highway was solid with them.

"There come some more," said Carmack.

The two policemen looked at the crowd of people walking toward the beach. Many of them talked and laughed. Some of them were very quiet and serious. But they all walked toward the beach.

Reordon shook his head. "I don't get it," he said for the hundreth time that week. "I just don't get it."

Carmack shrugged.

"Don't think about it," he said. "It's happening. What else is there?"

"But it's *crazy*."

"Well, there they go," said Carmack.

As the two policemen watched, the crowd of people moved across the gray sands of the beach and walked into the water. Some of them started swimming. Most of them couldn't because of their clothes. Carmack saw a young woman flailing at the water and dragged down by the fur coat she was wearing.

In several minutes they were all gone. The two policemen stared at the place where the people had walked into the water.

"How long does it go on?" Reordon asked.

"Until they're gone, I guess," said Carmack.

"But *why?*"

"You ever read about the lemmings?" Carmack asked.

"No."

"They're rodents who live in the Scandinavian countries. They keep breeding until all their food supply is gone. Then they move across the country, ravaging everything in their way. When they reach the sea they keep going. They swim until their strength is gone. Millions of them."

"You think that's what *this* is?" asked Reordon.

"Maybe," said Carmack.

"People aren't rodents!" Reordon said angrily.

Carmack didn't answer.

They stood on the edge of the highway waiting but nobody appeared.

"Where are they?" asked Reordon.

"Maybe they've all gone in," Carmack said.

"*All* of them?"

"It's been going on for more than a week," Carmack said. "People could have gotten here from all over. Then there are the lakes."

Reordon shuddered. "All of them," he said.

"I don't know," said Carmack, "but they've been coming right along until now."

"Oh, God," said Reordon.

Carmack took out a cigarette and lit it. "Well," he said, "what now?"

Reordon sighed. "Us?" he said.

"You go," Carmack said. "I'll wait a while and see if there's anyone else."

"All right." Reordon put his hand out. "Goodbye, Carmack," he said.

They shook hands. "Goodbye, Reordon," Carmack said.

He stood smoking his cigarette and watching his friend walk across the gray sand of the beach and into the water until it was over his head. He saw Reordon swim a few dozen yards before he disappeared.

After a while he put out his cigarette and looked around. Then he walked into the water too.

A million cars stood empty along the beach.

THE EDGE

It was almost two before there was a chance for lunch. Until then his desk was snow-banked with demanding papers, his telephone rang constantly and an army of insistent visitors attacked his walls. By twelve, his nerves were pulled like violin strings knobbed to their tightest. By one, the strings drew close to shearing; by one-thirty they began to snap. He had to get away; now, immediately; flee to some shadowy restaurant booth, have a cocktail and leisurely meal; listen to somnolent music. He had to.

Down on the street, he walked beyond the zone of eating places he usually frequented, not wishing to risk seeing anyone he knew. About a quarter of a mile from the office he found a cellar restaurant named Franco's. At his request, the hostess led him to a rear booth where he ordered a martini; then, as the woman turned away, he stretched out his legs beneath the table and closed his eyes. A grateful sigh murmured from him. This was the ticket. Dimlit comfort, Muzak thrumming at the bottom fringe of audibility, a curative drink. He sighed again. A few more days like this, he thought, and I'm gone.

"Hi, Don."

He opened his eyes in time to see the man drop down across from him. "How goes it?" asked the man.

"What?" Donald Marshall stared at him.

"Gawd," said the man. "What a day, what a day." He grinned tiredly. "You, too?"

"I don't believe—" began Marshall.

"*Ah*," the man said, nodding, pleased, as a waitress brought the martini. "That for me. Another, please; dryer than dry."

"Yes, sir," said the waitress and was gone.

"There," said the man, stretching. "No place like Franco's for getting away from it all, eh?"

"Look here," said Marshall, smiling awkwardly. "I'm afraid you've made a mistake."

"Hmmm?" The man leaned forward, smiling back.

"I say I'm afraid you've made a mistake."

"I have?" The man grunted. "What'd I do, forget to shave? I'm liable to. No?" he said as Marshall frowned. "Wrong tie?"

"You don't understand," said Marshall.

"What?"

Marshall cleared his throat. "I'm—not who you think I am," he said.

"Huh?" The man leaned forward again, squinting. He straightened up, chuckling. "What's the story, Don?" he asked.

Marshall fingered at the stem of his glass. "Yes, what is the story?" he said, less politely now.

"I don't get you," said the man.

"Who do you think I am?" asked Marshall, his voice rising a little.

The man began to speak, gaped a trifle, then began to speak again. "What do you mean who do I—?" He broke off as the waitress brought the second martini. They both sat quietly until she was gone.

"Now," said the man curiously.

"Look, I'm not going to accuse you of anything," said Marshall, "but you don't know me. You've never met me in your whole life."

"I don't—!" The man couldn't finish; he looked flabbergasted. "*I don't know you?*" he said.

Marshall had to laugh. "Oh, this is ludicrous," he said.

The man smiled appreciatively. "I knew you were ribbing me," he admitted, "but—" He shook his head. "You had me going there for a second."

Marshall put down his glass, the skin beginning to tighten across his cheeks.

"I'd say this had gone about far enough," he said. "I'm in no mood for—"

"*Don*," the man broke in. "What's wrong?"

Marshall drew in a deep breath, then let it waver out. "Oh, well," he said, "I suppose it's an honest mistake." He forced a smile. "Who *do* you think I am?"

The man didn't answer. He looked at Marshall intently.

"*Well?*" asked Marshall, beginning to lose patience.

"This isn't a joke?" said the man.

"Now, look—"

"No, wait, wait," said the man, raising one hand.

"I . . . suppose it's possible there could be two men who look so much alike they—"

He stopped abruptly and looked at Marshall. "Don, you're *not* ribbing me, are you?"

"Now listen to me—!"

"All right, I apologize," said the man. He sat gazing at Marshall for a moment; then he shrugged and smiled perplexedly. "I could have sworn you were Don Marshall," he said.

Marshall felt something cold gathering around his heart.

"I am," he heard himself say.

The only sound in the restaurant was that of the music and the delicate clink of silverware.

"What is this?" asked the man.

"You tell me," said Marshall in a thin voice.

"You—" The man looked carefully at him. "This is not a joke," he said.

"Now see here!"

"All right, all right." The man raised both his hands in a conciliatory gesture. "It's not a joke. You claim I don't know you. All right. Granting that leaves us with—with *this*: a man who not only looks exactly like my friend but has exactly the same name. Is this possible?"

"Apparently so," said Marshall.

Abruptly, he picked up his glass and took momentary escape in the martini. The man did the same. The waitress came for their orders and Marshall told her to come back later.

"What's your name?" he asked then.

"Arthur Nolan," said the man.

Marshall gestured conclusively. "I don't know you," he said. There was a slight loosening of tension in his stomach.

The man leaned back and stared at Marshall. "This is fantastic," he said. He shook his head. "Utterly fantastic."

Marshall smiled and lowered his eyes to the glass.

"Where do you work?" asked the man.

"American-Pacific Steamship," Marshall answered, glancing up. He felt a beginning of enjoyment in himself. This was certainly something to take one's mind off the wrack of the day.

The man looked examiningly at him; and Marshall sensed the enjoyment fading.

Suddenly the man laughed.

"You must have had one sweet hell of a morning, buddy," he said.

"What?"

"No more," said the man.

"Listen—"

"I capitulate," said Nolan, grinning. "You're curdling my gin."

"Listen to me, damn it!" snapped Marshall.

The man looked startled. His mouth fell open and he put his drink down. "Don, what is it?" he asked, concerned now.

"You do not know me," said Marshall, very carefully. "I do not know you. Will you kindly accept that?"

The man looked around as if for help. Then he leaned in close and spoke, his voice soft and worried.

"Don, listen. Honestly. You don't know me?"

Marshall drew in a deep breath, teeth clenched against rising fury. The man drew back. The look on his face was, suddenly, frightening to Marshall.

"One of us is out of his mind," Marshall said. The levity he'd intended never appeared in his voice.

Nolan swallowed raggedly. He looked down at his drink as if unable to face the other man.

Marshall suddenly laughed. "Dear Lord," he said, "what a scene. You really think you know me, don't you?"

The man grimaced. "The Don Marshall I know," he said, "also works for American-Pacific."

Marshall shuddered. "That's impossible," he said.

"No," said the man flatly.

For a moment Marshall got the notion that this was some sort of insidious plot against him; but the distraught expression on the man's face weakened the suspicion. He took a sip of his martini, then, carefully, set down the glass and laid his palms on the table as if seeking the re-inforcement of its presence.

"American-Pacific Steamship Lines?" he asked.

The man nodded once. "Yes."

Marshall shook his head obdurately. "No," he said. "There's no other Marshall in our office. Unless," he added, quickly, "one of our clerks downstairs—"

"You're an—" The man broke off nervously. "He's an executive," he said.

Marshall drew his hands in slowly and put them in his lap. "Then I don't understand," he said. He wished, instantly, he hadn't said it.

"This . . . man told you he worked there?" he asked quickly.

"Yes."

"Can you prove he works there?" Marshall challenged, his voice breaking. "Can you prove his name is really Don Marshall?"

"Don, I—"

"Well, *can* you?"

"Are you married?" asked the man.

Marshall hesitated. Then, clearing his throat, he said, "I am."

Nolan leaned forward. "To Ruth Foster?" he asked.

Marshall couldn't hide his involuntary gasp.

"Do you live on the Island?" Nolan pressed.

"Yes," said Marshall weakly, "but—"

"In Huntington?"

Marshall hadn't even the strength to nod.

"Did you go to Columbia University?"

"*Yes*, but—" His teeth were on edge now.

"Did you graduate in June, nineteen forty?"

"No!" Marshall clutched at this. "I graduated in January, nineteen forty-one. Forty-*one!*"

"Were you a lieutenant in the Army?" asked Nolan, paying no attention.

Marshall felt himself slipping. "Yes," he muttered, "but you said—"

"*In the Eighty-Seventh Division?*"

"Now wait a minute!" Marshall pushed aside the nearly empty glass as if to make room for his rebuttal. "I can give you two very good explanations for this . . .

this fool confusion. One: a man who looks like me and knows a few things about me is pretending to be me; Lord knows why. Two: you know about me and you're trying to snare me into something. No, you can argue all you like!" he persisted, almost frantically, as the man began to object. "You can ask all the questions you like; but I know who I am and I know who I know!"

"Do you?" asked the man. He looked dazed.

Marshall felt his legs twitch sharply.

"Well, I have no intention of s-sitting here and arguing with you," he said. "This entire thing is absurd. I came here for some peace and quiet—a place I've never even been to before and—"

"*Don, we eat here all the time.*" Nolan looked sick.

"That's nonsense!"

Nolan rubbed a hand across his mouth. "You . . . you actually think this is some kind of *con* game?" he asked.

Marshall stared at him. He could feel the heavy pulsing of his heart.

"Or that—*my God*—that there's a man impersonating you? Don . . ." The man lowered his eyes. "I think—well, if I were you," he said quietly, "I'd—go to a doctor, a—"

"Let's stop this, shall we?" Marshall interrupted coldly.

"I suggest one of us leave." He looked around the restaurant. "There's plenty of room in here."

He turned his eyes quickly from the man's stricken face and picked up his martini. "Well?" he said.

The man shook his head. "Dear God," he murmured.

"I said let's stop it," Marshall said through clenched teeth.

"That's it?" asked Nolan, incredulously. "You're willing to—to let it go at that?"

Marshall started to get up.

"No, no, wait," said Nolan. "I'll go." He stared at Marshall blankly. "I'll go," he repeated.

Abruptly, he pushed to his feet as if there were a leaden mantle around his shoulders.

"I don't know what to say," he said, "but—for God's sake, Don—see a doctor."

He stood by the side of the booth a moment longer, looking down at Marshall. Then, hastily, he turned and walked toward the front door. Marshall watched him leave.

When the man had gone he sank back against the booth wall and stared into his drink. He picked up the toothpick and mechanically stirred the impaled onion around in the glass. When the waitress came he ordered the first item he saw on the menu.

While he ate he thought about how insane it had been. For, unless the man Nolan was a consummate actor, he had been sincerely upset by what had happened.

What *had* happened? An out-and-out case of mistaken identity was one thing. A mistaken identity which seemed not quite wholly mistaken was another. How had the man known these things about him? About Ruth, Huntington, American-Pacific, even his lieutenancy in the 87th Division? *How?*

Suddenly, it struck him.

Years ago he'd been a devotee of fantastic fiction—stories which dealt with trips to the moon, with traveling through time, with all of that. And one of the ideas used repeatedly was that of the alternate universe: a lunatic theory which stated that for every possibility there was a separate universe. Following this theory there might, conceivably, be a universe in which he knew this Nolan, ate at Franco's with him regularly and had graduated from Columbia a semester earlier.

It was absurd, really, yet there it was. What if, in entering Franco's, he had, accidentally, entered a universe one jot removed from the one he'd existed in at the office?

What if, the thought expanded, people were, without knowing it, continually entering these universes one jot removed? What if he himself had continually entered them and never known until today—when, in an accidental entry, he had gone one step too far?

He closed his eyes and shuddered. Dear Lord, he thought; dear, heavenly Lord, I *have* been working too hard. He felt as if he were standing at the edge of a cliff waiting for someone to push him off. He tried hard not to think about his talk with Nolan. If he thought about it he'd have to fit it into the pattern. He wasn't prepared to do that yet.

After a while, he paid his check and left the restaurant, the food like cold lead in his stomach. He cabbed to Pennsylvania Station and, after a short wait, boarded a North Shore train. All the way to Huntington, he sat in the smoker car staring out at the passing countryside, an unlit cigarette between his fingers. The heavy pressure in his stomach wouldn't go away.

When Huntington was reached, he walked across the station to the cab stand and, deliberately, got into one of them.

"Take me home, will you?" he looked intently at the driver.

"Sure thing, Mr. Marshall," said the driver, smiling.

Marshall sank back with a wavering sigh and closed his eyes. There was a tingling at his fingertips.

"You're home early," said the driver. "Feeling poorly?"

Marshall swallowed. "Just a headache," he said.

"Oh, I'm sorry."

As he rode home, Marshall kept staring at the town, despite himself, looking for discrepancies, for *differences*. But there were none; everything was just the same. He felt the pressure letting up.

Ruth was in the living room, sewing.

"*Don.*" She stood and hurried to him. "Is something wrong?"

"No, no," he said, putting down his hat. "Just a headache."

"Oh." She led him, sympathetically, to a chair and helped him off with his suitcoat and shoes. "I'll get you something right away," she said.

"Fine." When she was gone upstairs, Marshall looked around the familiar room and smiled at it. It was all right now.

Ruth was coming down the stairs when the telephone rang. He started up, then fell back again as she called, "I'll get it, darling."

"All right," he said.

He watched her in the hallway as she picked up the receiver and said hello. She listened. "Yes, darling," she said automatically. "You—"

Then she stopped and, holding out the receiver, stared at it as if it were something monstrous in her hand.

She put it back to her ear. "You . . . won't be home until late?" she asked in a faint voice.

Marshall sat there gaping at her, the beats of his heart like someone striking at him. Even when she turned to look at him, the receiver lowered in her hand, he couldn't turn away. Please, he thought. Please don't say it. *Please.*

"*Who are you?*" she asked.

A VISIT TO SANTA CLAUS

All the way across the dark parking lot, Richard kept whining sulkily.

"All right, that's e-*nough*," Helen said to him when they reached the car. "We'll see him on Tuesday. How many times do I have to tell you?"

"Wanna see 'im *now*," Richard said, twitching with a sob.

Ken was reaching for the keys, trying not to drop the packages in his arms. "*Oh*," he said irritably, "I'll take him."

"What do you mean?" she asked, shifting her bundles and shivering in the cold wind that raced across the car-packed lot.

"I mean I'll take him now," he said, fumbling for the door lock.

"*Now?*" she asked. "It's too late now. Why didn't you take him while we were in the store? There was plenty of time then."

"So I'll take him now. What's the difference?"

"I wanna see *Sanna* Claus!" Richard broke in, looking intently at Helen. "Mama, I wanna see Sanna Claus *now!*"

"Not now, Richard," Helen said, shaking her head. She dumped her bundles on the front seat and straightened her arms with a groan. "That's *e-nough*, I said," she warned as Richard began whining again. "Mommy's too tired to walk all the way back to the store."

"You don't have to go," Ken told her, throwing his packages in beside hers. "I'll take him in myself." He turned on the light.

"Mama, *please*, Mama? *Please?*"

She made herself a place on the seat and sank down with a weary grunt. He noticed the lock of unkempt brown hair dangling across her forehead, the caking dryness of her lipstick.

"Well, what made you change your mind now?" she asked tiredly. "I only asked you about a hundred times to take him while we were in the store."

"For God's sake, what's the difference?" he snapped. "Do you want to drive back here on Tuesday just to see Santa Claus?"

"No."

"Well, then. . . ." He noticed the wrinkles in her stockings as she pulled her legs around and faced the front of the car. She looked old and sour in the dim light. It gave him an odd sensation in his stomach.

"*Please*, Mama?" Richard was begging as if Helen were all authority, Ken thought, as if *he*, the father, had no say at all. Well, that was probably the way it was.

Helen stared glumly at the windshield, then reached back and turned off the light. Two hours of being exposed to frantic Christmas shoppers, nerve-strained sales people, Richard's constant demands to see Santa Claus, and Ken's irritating refusals to take him had jaded her.

"And what am I supposed to do while you're gone?" she asked.

"It'll only be a few minutes, for God's sake," Ken answered. He'd been on hooks all night, either remote and uncommunicative or snapping nervously at her and Richard.

"Oh, go a-*head*," she said, arranging the coat over her legs, "and please hurry."

"*Sanna* Claus, *Sanna* Claus!" Richard shouted, tugging joyously at his father's topcoat.

"All right!" Ken flared. "Stop pulling at me, for God's sake!"

"Joy to the world. The Lord has come," Helen said, her sigh one of disgust.

"Yeah, sure," Ken said bitterly, grabbing at Richard's hand. "Come on."

Helen pulled the car door shut, and Ken noticed she didn't push down the button to lock it. She might though, after they'd gone. *The keys!*—the thought exploded suddenly, and he drove his hand into his topcoat pocket, his palsied fingers tightening over their cold metal. A dry swallow moved his throat and he sucked in cold air shakily, heartbeats thudding like a fist inside his chest. Take it easy, he told himself, just . . . take it easy.

He knew enough not to look back. It would be like taking one more look at a funeral. He stared up, deliberately, at the glittering neon wreath on the department store roof. He could barely feel Richard's hand on his. His other hand clutched at the keys in his pocket. He wouldn't look back, he—

"Ken!"

His body clamped in a spasmodic start as her voice rang out thinly in the huge lot. Automatically, he turned and saw her standing by the Ford, looking at them.

"Leave the keys!" she called. "I'll drive around to the front of the store so you don't have to walk all the way back here!"

He stared blankly at her, feeling the sudden cramped tightness of his stomach muscles.

"That's—" He cleared his throat, almost furiously. "It's not that far!" he called back.

He turned away before she could answer, noticing how Richard glanced at him. His heartbeat was like a club swung against the wall of his chest.

"Mama's calling," Richard said.

"You want to see Santa Claus or not?" Ken demanded sharply.

"Y-es."

"Then shut up!"

He swallowed again painfully and lengthened his

stride. Why did *that* have to happen? A shudder ran down his back. He looked up at the neon wreath again, but he could still see Helen standing by the car in her green corduroy coat, one arm raised a little, her eyes on him. He could still hear her voice—*so you don't have to walk all the way back here!*—sounding thin and plaintive over the buffeting night wind.

He felt that wind chilling his cheeks now as his and Richard's shoes made a crisp, uneven sound on the gravel-strewn asphalt. Seventy yards, maybe it was seventy yards to the store. Was that the sound of their car door slamming shut? She was probably angry. If she pushed down the button, it would be harder to—

The man in the dark, sagging-brimmed hat stood at the end of the aisle. Ken pretended not to see him, but the air seemed rarefied suddenly, as though he were beyond atmosphere, trudging in an icy darkness that was nearly vacuum. It was the constriction around his heart that made him feel that way, the apparent inability of his lungs to hold in breath.

"Does Sanna Claus love me?" Richard asked.

Ken's chest labored with forced breathing. "Yes, yes," he said, "he—does." The man just stood there staring up at the sky, both hands deep in the pockets of his old checked overcoat, as if he were waiting for his wife to come out of the department store. But he wasn't. Ken's fingers grew rigid on the keys. His legs felt like heavy wood carrying him closer to the man.

I won't do it, he thought suddenly. He'd walk right by the man, take Richard to see Santa Claus, return to the car, go home, forget about it. He felt incapable and without strength. Helen alone in the Ford, sitting beside their Christmas packages, waiting for her husband and son to return. The thought sent strange electric prick-lings through his body. I just won't do it. He heard the words as if someone were speaking them in his mind. I just won't—

His hand was growing cold and numb on the keys as, unconscious of it, he cut off the flow of blood to his fingers.

He *had* to do it; it was the only way. He wasn't going to return to the nerve-knotting frustration that was his present, the dreary expanse that was his future. Interior rages were poisoning him. For his own health it had to be done, for what was left of his life.

They reached the end of the aisle and walked past the man.

Richard cried, "Daddy, you dropped the keys!"

"Come on!" He pulled at Richard's hand, forcing himself not to look back over his shoulder.

"But you did, Daddy!"

"I said—!"

Ken's voice broke off abruptly as Richard pulled away from him and ran to where the ring of keys lay on the asphalt. He stared with helpless eyes at the man who hadn't budged from his place. The man appeared to shrug, but Ken couldn't see what his expression was beneath the wide hat brim.

Richard came running back with the keys. "Here, Daddy."

Ken slid them into his topcoat pocket with shaking fingers, a sick dismay twisting his insides. It won't work, he thought, feeling both an agony of disappointment and an agony of wrenching guilt.

"Say thank you," Richard said, taking his father's hand again.

Ken stood motionless in indecision, still holding on to the keys in his pocket. Empathic muscle tension pulled him toward the man, but he knew he couldn't go to him. Richard would see.

"Let's go, Daddy," Richard urged.

Ken turned away quickly, his face a painted mask as

he started for the store. He felt dizzy, without feeling. It's over! he thought in bitter fury, *over!*

"Say thank you, Daddy."

"Will you——!" The sound of his voice startled him and he trapped the hysterical surge of words behind pressed, trembling lips. Richard was silent. He glanced cautiously at his taut-faced father.

They were halfway to the store entrance when the man in the checked overcoat brushed past Ken.

"'Scuse it," muttered the man, and apparently by accident his arm brushed roughly against the pocket where the keys were, indicating that he wanted and was ready to receive them.

Then the man was past them, walking in jerky strides toward the store. Ken watched him go, feeling as if his head were being compressed between two hands, the palms contoured to his skull. It's not over, he thought. He didn't even know whether he was glad it wasn't. He saw the man stop and turn before one of the glass doors that flanked the revolving door. Now, he told himself, it has to be now. He took out the keys again.

"I wanna go that way, Daddy!" Richard was tugging him toward the revolving door which spun shoppers into the crowded din or out into the silent chill of night.

"It's too crowded," he heard himself say, but it was someone else speaking. It's my future, he kept thinking, my future.

"It's not crowded, Daddy!"

He didn't argue. He jerked Richard toward the side door. And as he pulled the door open with the keys in his hand, he felt them grabbed from his fingers.

Then, in a second, he and Richard were in the noisome brightness of the store, and it was done.

Ken didn't look over his shoulder, but he knew the man was walking back into the dark lot now, back toward the aisle where the Ford was parked.

For one horrible instant, he felt as if he were going to make an outcry. A great sickness rushed up through his body, and he almost yelled and dashed back into the night after the man. No, I've changed my mind; I don't want it done! In that instant, everything he hated about Helen and his life with her seemed to vanish, and all he could remember was that she was going to drive the car to the front of the store so he and Richard wouldn't have to walk back across the cold, wind-swept lot.

But then Richard had pulled him into the warmth and the noise and the milling press of shoppers and he was walking along dizzily, moving deeper into the store.

Chimes were playing from the second-floor balcony—
Joy to the world, the Lord has come. She'd said that. He
felt dizzy and ill; sweat began trickling across his forehead. He couldn't go back now.

He stopped in the middle of the floor and leaned
against a pillar, his legs feeling as if they'd turned to
water. It's too late, he thought, too late. There was nothing he could do now.

"I wanna see Sanna Claus, Daddy."

Breath faltered through his parted lips. "Yes," he said,
nodding feebly. "All right."

He tried to move along without thinking but found
that impossible. His thoughts were flashing visual im-
ages. The man walking down the wide aisle toward the
Ford. The man checking the miniature license plate on
the key ring to make sure he got the right car. The man's
face as it had been that night in the Main Street bar—
thin, pale, corrupted. A whimper started in Ken's throat,
but he cut it off. *Helen*, his thought said with anguish.

THIS WAY TO SANTA'S MAGIC HOUSE! He started numbly
toward the down escalator, Richard skipping and wrig-
gling beside him, whispering in breathless excitement,
"*Sanna* Claus, *Sanna* Claus." What would Richard feel
when his mother was—

All right!—he forced a strengthening rage through himself—if he had to think, he'd think about the future, not this. He hadn't planned all this just to collapse into useless infirmity when it came about. There was reason behind the act; it wasn't just a thoughtless viciousness.

They stepped onto the escalator. Richard's hand was tight in his, but he hardly felt it. South America and Rita—he'd think about that. Twenty-five thousand dollars insurance money; the girl he'd wanted at college and never stopped wanting; a future without the debasing struggle to stay one jump ahead of creditors. Freedom, simple pleasures and a relationship that wouldn't be eroded away by the abrasion of petty existence.

The up escalator angled past them, and Ken glanced at the shoppers' faces—tired, irritable, happy, blank. *It came upon a midnight clear*, the chimes began to play. He stared straight ahead, thinking about Rita and South America. Thinking about that made everything a lot easier.

Now the chimes faded and were swallowed in a raucous glee club blaring of "Jingle Bells." Richard began skipping excitedly as they stepped off the escalator, and Ken suddenly found himself thinking about Helen again. *Jingle all the way!*

"There 'e is!" Richard cried, pulling frantically. "There!"

"All right, all right!" Ken muttered under his breath as they moved toward the line that shuffled toward Santa's Magic House.

Had it happened yet? That contracting of stomach muscle again. Was the man in the car? Was Helen unconscious in back? Was the man driving across the lot toward dark side streets where he'd—?

Don't worry. The man's last words to him were like a flame searing his mind. *Don't worry. I'll make it look good.*

Look good, look good, look good, look good. The words thumped on in his thoughts as he and Richard moved slowly toward the house of Santa Claus. One hundred down, nine hundred to follow—the price of one medium-sized wife.

Ken shut his eyes suddenly and felt himself shivering as if it were cold in the store instead of unbearably stuffy. His head ached. Drops of sweat trickled down from his arm pits, feeling like insects on his flesh. It's too late, he thought, realizing that part of the tension he'd felt since entering the store had been the struggle with his impulse to rush back to the car to stop the man.

But, as you say—he heard a quiet voice whispering in his mind—it's too late.

"What shall I tell Sanna, Daddy?" Richard asked.

Ken looked down bleakly at his five-year-old son and thought, he'll be better off with Helen's mother—a lot better off. I can't—

"What shall I, Daddy?"

He tried to smile, and for a moment he even managed to visualize himself as a gallant man bearing up under a terrible burden that fate had put on his shoulders.

"Tell him—what you want for Christmas," he said. "Tell him you've been a—a good boy and . . . what you want for Christmas. That's all."

"But how?"

The vision had already faded; he knew exactly what he was and what he'd done.

"How should I know?" he snapped angrily. "Look, if you don't want to see him, you don't have to."

A man in front of them turned and shook his head at Ken with a wry smile that seemed to say, I know what you're going through, buddy. Ken's smile in return was little more than a slight, mirthless twitching of the lips. Oh, God, I've got to get out of here, he thought miserably. How can I stand here while—

Breath labored in his lungs. It was what he had to do.

It was the plan and it had to be carried out. He wasn't going to spoil it now with stupid histrionics.

If only he could be with Rita, though, in her apartment, beside her. But it was impossible. He'd settle for a drink, a stiff one. Anything to break the tension.

They pushed open the white gate and it set off a record of a man's booming laughter. Ken jumped and looked around. The laughter sounded insane to him. He tried not to listen, but it surrounded him, dinning in his ears.

Then the gate closed behind them and the laughter stopped. He heard a thin voice piping over the PA system, *I wiss you a mehwy Cwiss-muss an' a Happ-ee New Year.*

I'll make it look good.

Ken released Richard. He rubbed his damp palm against his coat. Richard tried to take his hand again, but Ken jerked his hand away so savagely that Richard looked frightened and puzzled.

No. No, I can't act this way, Ken heard the instruction in his mind. Richard might be asked questions, questions like *How did your daddy act when you were in the store together?* He took Richard's hand and managed to force a smile.

"Almost there," he said. The calmness of his voice shocked him. I tell you I don't know how I lost the keys. I had them in my pocket when I went in the store; I'm sure of it. That's all I know. Are you trying to imply that—?

No! ALL WRONG. No matter what they intimated he must never let them know he understood. Shocked, dazed, hardly capable of coherence—that was the way he'd have to be. A man who had taken his son to see Santa Claus, who had been told the next day that they'd found his wife still in the car.

I'll make it look—Why couldn't he forget that!

The Santa Claus was sitting in a high-backed chair on the porch of the magic house—magic because it changed color every fifteen seconds. He was a fat, middle-aged man with a chuckling voice who held children on his lap a few moments, spoke the formula words, then put the children down, one peppermint stick richer, patted them on the rear and said goodbye and Merry Christmas.

When Richard came on the porch, Santa Claus picked him up and set him on his broad, red-knickered lap. Ken stood on the bottom step, feeling dizzy in the warmth of the store, staring, dull-eyed, at the red-rouged face, the dreadfully false whiskers.

"Well, sonny," said Santa Claus, "have you been a good boy this year?"

Richard tried to answer, but speech stuck in his throat. Ken saw him nod, flushing nervously. *He'll be better off with Helen's mother. I can't do right by him. I'd just—*

His eyes strained into focus on the red, whiskered face. "What?"

"I say has this boy been good this year?"

"Oh. Yes. *Yes.* Very good."

"Well," said Santa Claus, "old Santa is glad to hear that. Very glad. And what would you like for Christmas, sonny?"

Ken stood there, motionless, sweat soaking into his shirt while the faint voice of his son droned on endlessly, itemizing toys he wanted. The porch seemed to waver before his eyes. *I'm sick,* he thought. *I've got to get out of here and get some fresh air. Helen, I'm sorry, I'm sorry. I . . . just couldn't do it any other way, don't you see?*

Then Richard came down the steps with his peppermint stick, and they started toward the escalator.

"Sanna said I'll get *ev'*rything I ast," Richard told him.

Ken nodded jerkily, reaching into his suit coat pocket for a handkerchief. *Maybe the people wouldn't think it* was perspiration he was wiping from his cheeks. Maybe they'd think he was overcome with emotion because it was Christmas and he loved Christmas and that's why there were tears on his face.

"I'm gonna tell Mama," Richard said.

"Yes." His voice was barely audible. We'll go out and walk back to where the car was parked. We'll look around a while. Then I'll call the police.

"Yes," he said.

"What, Daddy?"

He shook his head. "Nothing."

The escalator lifted them toward the main floor. The glee club started singing "Jingle Bells" again. Ken stood behind Richard and stared down at his blond hair. This is the part that counts most, he told himself. What went before was just time consumption.

He'd have to act surprised on the telephone, irritated. A little concerned, maybe, but not too much. A man wouldn't panic under such circumstances. Normally, a man wouldn't conceive that his wife's disappearance meant—Behind them the recorded laughter boomed faintly over the glee club's singing.

He tried to erase his mind as if it were a blackboard,

but words kept forming there. Be a little concerned, a little irritated, a—

—We're not implying anything Mister Burns. Abruptly, they were at him again. We're just saying that twenty-five thousand is a lot of insurance.

Look! His face tightened as he flared back at them. It's something we believed in, see? I'm insured for twenty-five thousand, too, you know. You forget that.

It was his biggest point. The insurance had been in effect less than a year, but at least they were both equally insured.

He scuffed his shoe toe at the top of the escalator and found himself back in the store again, walking beside his son toward the doors which would revolve them into the night. A thin current of air fluttered his trouser cuffs. He felt the chill on his ankles. We'll look around a while, then I'll—

It came over him. He didn't know how, but suddenly he couldn't leave the store. Suddenly he was standing in front of a counter, staring down intently at hand-kerchiefs and ties. He felt Richard's eyes on him and he was admonishing himself, I mustn't look upset! I didn't plan all this just to break down at the last minute!

Rita. South America. Money. It was good to think about the future. He'd known that all along, and yet he'd allowed himself to forget. The future was what was important, Rita and he together in South America.

There, that was better. He took in a long, faltering breath of warm air. The hands in his coat pockets unknotted.

"Come on," he said, and this time he was grimly pleased at the calmness of his voice. "Let's go."

As he took Richard's hand, the closing gong sounded above the organ playing "Silent Night, Holy Night." Perfect timing, he told himself. Nine p.m., Monday night. We'll go out to where the Ford was parked; then I'll call the police.

But should he call the police? A momentary touch of panic startled him. Wouldn't he, normally, think that maybe Helen had gotten angry and—

I thought she'd gotten angry and driven home without us. No, she's never done anything like it before. Anyway we went home by bus, my son and I, but my wife wasn't there. And I don't know where she is. Yes, I checked at her mother's house. No, that's our only relative in the city.

They had pushed through the doorway now and were

back outside. Ken looked straight across the car-filled lot as they moved away from the store. He couldn't feel the grip of Richard's hand in his. All he could feel was his heartbeat, leaping—like something imprisoned—at the wall of his chest. Well, I wonder where Mother went, he imagined himself saying to Richard when they'd reach the place where the Ford had been parked. Where's Mama? would be Richard's reply. Then there would be the wait, calling the police finally. No, she's never done anything like this, his mind ticked on, unbidden. I assumed she was angry and had gone home, but when my son and I got home she wasn't there.

For a moment, he thought that he had died, that his heart had ceased to beat. He felt as if he'd been turned to stone. The wind blew coldly into his stricken face.

"Come on, Daddy," Richard said, tugging at him.

He didn't move. He stood looking at the car, Helen sitting in it.

"I'm cold, Daddy."

He found himself walking, moving with a dazed, somnambulistic tread. Intelligence would not return to him. He could only stare at the car and at Helen and suffer a twisting sickness in his stomach. His head felt light and fragile, as if it were about to float off. Only the impact of his footsteps that jarred consciousness through him held the parts of his body together. His eyes were set unmovingly on the car. He knew a great, warm surge of relief. Helen was looking at him.

He pulled open the door.

"It's about *time* you got back," she said.

He couldn't speak. Trembling, he pushed the seat forward and Richard clambered into the back.

"Come on, come *on*. Let's get out of here," Helen said.

Ken slid his hand into his coat pocket and with the act remembered.

"Well?" she said.

"I—I—can't find the keys." He patted feebly at his pockets. "Had them with me when—"

"Oh, *no*." The lilt of her voice was weariness and disgust.

Ken swallowed.

"Well, where are they?" Helen asked. "I swear if your head weren't fastened to your shoulders—"

"I—I don't know," he said. "I—must have dropped them—somewhere."

"Well, go pick them *up* then," she snapped.

"Yes," he said, "yes." He pushed the door out almost desperately and stood in the cold air.

"I'll be right back," he said.

She didn't answer, but he could feel her hostility.

He shut the door and moved away from the car, his face beginning to harden. That bastard, taking his money and—!

He suddenly imagined himself trying to explain the lack of a hundred dollars in the checking account. She'd never believe that it had simply vanished. She'd investigate, find out about the cash he'd gotten, probe, demand. Oh, God, he thought, I'm done, I'm *done*.

He looked off, his eyes unseeing, fixed on the huge neon wreath on the roof of the store. In the middle of it, tall, white letters were blinking off and on. He focused on them suddenly. MERRY CHRISTMAS—darkness. MERRY CHRISTMAS—darkness. MERRY CHRISTMAS—darkness.

DR. MORTON'S FOLLY

He had just finished sterilizing his dental tools when there was a loud knocking on the front office door. What on earth? Dr. Morton frowned. Who in the name of heaven would be showing up this time of night? He stood motionless, assuming that whoever it was would leave when no one responded.

Instead, the knocking persisted, getting louder. Dr. Morton sighed wearily. Can't they tell that the office is closed? he thought.

The knocking continued, starting to become belligerent. Damn. Did they know he was here because the room lights could be seen from the outside? He sighed again. He was tired, and he wanted to go home.

As the knocking went on, now with a kind of exaggerated righteous rhythm, Dr. Morton left the workroom and trudged slowly down the hall to the office door. He opened it and went inside. In a momentary silence between knocks, he said firmly, "*The office is closed.*"

A man replied, "I have to see you."

Dr. Morton exhaled tiredly. "I'm sorry," he said, "but we're closed for the night. You should have—"

"I *know* you're closed," the man interrupted. "This is an emergency. I'm in considerable pain."

Oh, dear God, Dr. Morton thought, the word had always gotten through to him. Considerable *pain?* He sighed in surrender. "One moment," he said. He unlocked the front door and opened it.

The man was tall and lean, wearing a black suit, his shirt white, his collar opened above a dark tie. Around his neck he wore a red silk scarf. His skin looked sallow.

He smiled at Dr. Morton. "I appreciate this," he said. "I realize that it's late, but as I said, I'm in considerable pain."

Dr. Morton withheld a fatigued sigh. "This way," he said, gesturing toward the office door.

"Thank you, sir," the man said.

His polite tone helped, somewhat, to ease Dr. Morton's aggravation. He followed the man into the hall, noticing how black the man's hair was. What's your name, Mr. Black? he thought, sarcastically.

"George Goodman," said the man.

Dr. Morton repressed a smile. No sooner asked than answered, he thought. Mr. Goodman. Hardly appropriate but possibly true.

"In there," he told the man, pointing toward the first workroom.

"Thank you, sir," the man said again.

So *polite*, thought Dr. Morton. Very nice. Or affected.

"Please sit down," he said.

"Thank you," said the man. Laying his red scarf on the right counter, he sat on the chair and elevated his legs. His shoes were black as well. As were his socks. *Goodman?* thought Dr. Morton. Totally inappropriate. Well, let it go. "I hope this won't take long," the man said.

"We'll see," Dr. Morton muttered. He fastened a cloth around the man's neck.

"So, what's the problem?" he asked.

In answer, the man opened his mouth and pointed inside. Dr. Morton put on his face mask and leaned in to examine the interior.

Good God! He could not control a gasp of startled revulsion.

"Something wrong?" the man asked.

"Well . . ." Dr. Morton hesitated. "Do you . . . brush your teeth very often?" he asked. He wanted to speak more directly but contained himself. The man's breath was shocking. With an ordinary patient, he would have demanded a cleaning before doing an examination. A pity Miss Jensen wasn't here or he might well have prescribed a cleaning before beginning. However . . . he certainly would not attempt a cleaning himself. Under the circumstances, absolutely not.

"I beg your pardon?" he said, realizing that Mr. Goodman (Lord, what an inappropriate name!) had answered his question.

"I *said*," the man said, "occasionally." He sounded offended. *I'm* the one who should be offended, Dr. Morton thought. Your breath is revolting.

"The *problem?*" the man reminded Dr. Morton.

The *problem* is I'd like you to get out of my office and

brush your damned teeth! Dr. Morton thought. But then . . . *pain.* He couldn't ignore that. No matter how atrocious the man's breath was.

Dr. Morton adjusted the overhead light and looked inside the man's mouth, trying not to breathe. Immediately, he saw the problem. "You have a badly decayed cavity in your left canine tooth," he said. He wanted to add that the tooth seemed abnormally long. But he'd already offended the man regarding his breath and didn't care to add to that. Probably runs in the family, he thought. Peculiar family.

"So what can be done about it?" the man inquired.

"*I* can't do anything," Dr. Morton said. "I can only advise you to have the tooth extracted by—"

"*No!*" the man said loudly; it sounded close to a snarl. It gave Dr. Morton a start.

"I'm sorry, but I see no other course," he said. "I believe the tooth should be extracted and, since I can't do it, I'd recommend Dr. Wellington, a most dependable oral surgeon—"

"What can *you* do, sir? *Now. Here,*" the man broke in.

Dr. Morton gazed at him intently. There was something menacing about Mr. Goodman. Something pathetic as well. The thought was validated as the man said, "*Please*, Doctor. Do whatever you can. I'm in dreadful pain."

That word again. Dr. Morton was totally vulnerable in its presence. He had to offer something.

"Sir?" the man said.

"Well . . ." Dr. Morton started.

"*Sir?*" the man demanded.

". . . might try—" Dr. Morton started again.

"*Yes?*"

Dr. Morton did not attempt to muffle a heavy sigh. What time was it anyway? Would he *ever* get home? Blanche was probably tired of waiting and already asleep in bed.

"*Sir?*" the man demanded again. Forcefully now.

"I could try to fill—the—" began Dr. Morton.

"*Good.*" The man cut him off. "*Do* it."

"I didn't finish." Dr. Morton said. "I can't guarantee anything. The cavity appears to be below the gum line. If it is—"

"*Please.*" The man cut him off again. "It doesn't matter where it is. *I need the tooth*."

"Well . . . *sir*." Dr. Morton spoke cajolingly. "The

tooth is valuable, certainly. All teeth are. But under the circumstances. The *condition* of the tooth . . ."

"I don't *care* what the condition of the tooth is!" the man said loudly. "I *need* it!"

Well . . . *damn* it, Dr. Morton thought. The man seemed adamant. What to do? He couldn't throw the man out. He didn't think that was possible anyway. Mr. Goodman—if that *was* his name—could be muscular. Dr. Morton exhaled openly.

The man watched him prepare an injection needle, filling it from the container of lidocaine.

"What are you doing?" he asked.

"Preparing a pain injection," Dr. Morton told him.

The man scowled. "No injection," he said.

"Mr. Goodman," objected Dr. Morton. "You cannot—"

"*No . . . injection.*" The man's voice was almost threatening.

Well, damn it! Dr. Morton thought. He just wouldn't do the filling then! Let the man endure the pain! He did not intend to drill that awful looking cavity without the aid of lidocaine! Absolutely not!

"*Please*, sir." The man was starting to plead. "*The pain*

is terrible." No further sense of threat. There were even tears in his eyes. Dear God. Dr. Morton felt guilty. He had to *try*, anyway. The poor man was in dreadful need, that was obvious.

"Oh, very well," he said.

"*Thank* you, sir." The man sounded genuinely grateful.

Just stop calling me sir, will you? Dr. Morton thought peevishly as he prepared the drill, thinking how more convenient it was for Miss Jensen to do all the preparatory work.

He braced himself. "I warn you," he told the man, "this is going to hurt. If you still—"

"*Drill,*" the man interrupted. "I'm ready."

So be it, Dr. Morton thought. Suffer, then. He felt a twinge of guilt at the unkind thought, then dropped it. He *had* offered lidocaine. If the man refused it, he had to be prepared for the worst. He'd likely strike the nerve. Heaven help the man then.

He began to drill.

At first, he assumed that, as a number of patients did, the man was resisting the commencement of pain. It wouldn't work without lidocaine. Mr. Goodman would soon be in agony. The anticipation was initially pleasing to Dr. Morton. The man had been little but difficult to treat. The satisfaction soon wavered, then disappeared however as he waited, almost tensely, for the first sign of pain from the man. The initial tightening of his cheeks, the involuntary clamping shut of his eyes, the uncontrollable hiss.

To his amazement none of the expected reactions took place. The man remained silent, gaze fixed on the ceiling. He never stirred, never showed a sign of distress. Dr. Morton couldn't understand it. He was drilling straight into the decay of the cavity. He had to be affecting the nerve. Was the man one of those rare people who never felt pain? Who could lay a palm on an open flame and never notice? Curious.

The man's mouth was beginning to fill with particled blood. Dr. Morton straightened up. "Rinse out," he said, gesturing toward the small round sink beside the chair. Lord, he thought. Already his back hurt. He'd been looking forward to going home, taking a hot shower, and getting into bed. No such luck.

He watched as the man picked up the paper cup and put some water in his mouth. His cheeks puffed out as he washed the bloody water around in his mouth. Patients didn't usually do that, Dr. Morton thought. They spit out what bloody cavity fragments and saliva were in their mouth, then rinsed out. Not this gentleman, of course. The idea vaguely amused him.

He started, eyes widening as the man swallowed again. Good God, thought Dr. Morton. "I didn't mean for you to *drink* it," he said, his voice unmanageably revulsed.

"It's all right," the man said.

"Well," Dr. Morton mumbled. What more was there to say? The man was more than intractable. He was disgusting.

Finish up, he told himself. Get this damned thing over with.

He continued drilling, making no attempt to avoid inflicting pain. It didn't seem to matter. The man remained stoic. Dr. Morton was repeatedly struck by that fact as the drill bit deep below the gum line. Ordinarily, even with the use of lidocaine, by now the average patient would be writhing with pain. Most of the time, he'd have to give them a second lidocaine shot and wait before continuing to drill.

Not with this man. He remained motionless, staring intently at the ceiling. When the bloody detritus collected in his throat, he swallowed it. Oh, for Christ's sake, Dr. Morton thought more than once.

At last, the drilling was concluded. As quickly as he could—Miss Jensen did it so much more efficiently—he mixed the filling and implanted it into the cavity with hard, abrupt movements.

"Don't chew on anything until this dries," he instructed.

"I won't," the man said.

Dr. Morton drew a deep breath. He wouldn't bother drying the filling. "Well, that's it then. It should hold," he said. He was about to add that he still believed the tooth should be extracted, but decided against it. He wanted the man out of here. He wanted to go home and relax.

"About the charge," the man said, rising from the chair.

"Call my secretary in the morning and give her your address," Dr. Morton said.

"I'll send you the money," the man replied.

"Fine." Dr. Morton's tone was impersonal.

He walked the man to the waiting room. There, instead of opening the front door, the man turned to face Dr. Morton.

"It was very kind of you," he said.

Think nothing of it, Dr. Morton felt inclined to say. I'm going to forget about it as soon as I can. "Thank you" was what he said.

The man smiled. He put a hand on each of Dr. Morton's shoulders. His grip was strong. It made Dr. Morton's shoulders hurt. "*Now*," said the man. His lips drew back from his teeth.

"Yes, the tooth looks fine," Dr. Morton said.

The man blinked, moved his lips forward, and withdrew his hands. "No," he said, "I may need you again."

Dr. Morton tightened. "I'm usually available," he said stiffly. The *nerve* of the man!

"Good," said the man. He opened the door and moved into the corridor.

Dr. Morton locked the door with a solid thrust. There, he thought. So much for you, Mr. Goodman. If that's really your name.

When he went back in the workroom to clean the drill, he saw the man's red scarf on the counter. Oh, no, he thought. He wasn't going to allow the man back to claim it. Snatching it off the counter, he left the room and hurried to the front door. Unlocking it, he pulled it open and lunged into the corridor. Here's your damn scarf! he thought of raging. He wouldn't, of course. But at least he'd be rid of Mr. Goodman. Peculiar—no, *weird*—Mr. Goodman.

He opened the front door of the building and stepped outside. Here's your scarf, sir! he said in his mind.

The parking lot was empty. Didn't the man drive here? Dr. Morton thought. Was he *walking?* At this time of night? Surely there was bus service available. A taxicab might not be possible.

He jerked back his head as a rushing sound moved overhead. A momentary shadow swept across him, making him start.

Quickly, Dr. Morton moved back into the building and walked to his office with unaccustomed speed. For some reason, he felt very cold.

THE WINDOW OF TIME

Let me say, at the outset, that I don't blame my daughter for what happened. Actually, "blame" is too critical a word. What I mean to say is that my daughter was hardly responsible for what happened. Miriam is a good soul, a benevolent human being. She never (well, almost never) found fault with my living in her home. And Bob's. And the three boys'. And if she did find fault, it was of such brief duration as to be negligible. Bob, on the other hand—well, let that go. (The main point

I want to make is that my daughter did not demean me in any way for my extended residence. She knew I was alone and friendless; all of them deceased, including my beloved wife, Agnes. Appreciating that, Miriam treated me with thoughtfulness, kindness. And, most importantly, love.)

So much for the outset. The upshot? I know that my daughter and her family were in a constant state of stress because of me. I did the best I could, using their second bathroom (I didn't have the temerity to utilize the master bathroom) as expeditiously as possible, watching television on the small black-and-white set in my bedroom, rarely watching the fifty-five-inch LCD color TV in their living room and sharing that only when we all agreed on a specific program. Most of my personal books were in storage and scarcely ever reread. I'd read them all anyway.

Oh, there were other elements of stress. Certain foods I couldn't eat. Medicine prescriptions I needed periodically. Rides to various doctors. (I'd lost my driver's license in 2008 following my stroke.) Well, why go on? I was, to be brief, in the way. So I decided to leave. I had enough private income from social security and my retirement pension from the Writers Guild. (I was rather a successful series television writer in the '60s and '70s.) So I had enough income to keep paying Miriam by the month even though I wasn't there.

I didn't tell her I was leaving. I knew she'd try to dissuade me. My age (eighty-two, I'd married late), my health (questionable), my need for company (beyond question). I didn't want to debate with her. So I just left, a parting note on the kitchen table. I didn't take any belongings with me. I could get them after I located a furnished room or flat. I waited until Miriam had gone shopping for groceries. Bob was at work (he's a car salesman, poor chap), the boys—Jeremy, seventeen, Arthur, fourteen, and Melvin, twelve—were at school. So I decamped from the three-bedroom, two-bath Kelsey domicile (Jeremy would likely be delighted at long last to acquire his own room) and walked over to Church Avenue. (Did I mention that their house was in the Flatbush section of Brooklyn? No, I didn't. Well, it is.) And I had seen (for some time) an ad in the local news sheet about a retirement home in that area called Golden Years. The name gave me the pip. Golden Years my foot! But I was in no position—or condition, for that matter—to go searching to hell and gone for an appropriate landing spot.

The home—I had trouble thinking of it as a "home"— was a couple of blocks west of Flatbush Avenue. The ad described it so. To be truthful, I can't tell east from west or north from south. I assumed that I was heading in the right direction and evidently, I was. I found the house a block and a half distant from what had been the RKO Kenmore Theatre in my youth. Not a bad-looking house, cleanly painted, a sign hanging above its porch which read G-LDEN YEARS, the *O* missing. No mention of retirement. I had to assume it was the place I was searching for.

No doorbell. Instead, a rather portentous-looking knocker made, I guessed, of cast iron painted to resemble copper. It made such a deafening resonance when I struck it against the door that it made me wince.

An old lady answered the door. My immediate assumption was that the house was hers and she was attempting to keep from losing it by renting out unused bedrooms.

She smiled at me. "You've come looking for a place," she said.

Her assumption would, ordinarily, have offended me.

But her demeanor was so friendly, her voice so agreeable, that I felt nothing but acceptance in her presence. "Yes, I am," I answered her. Politely.

"Come in then," she said, still smiling.

There was no mention of rental as she led me down the dimlit hall. Hung on both sides were old, faded photographs and paintings. *She must be almost my age*, I thought although I wouldn't have dreamed of asking. Her hair was silvery-gray, her clothes outdated, her dark dress ankle-length. She walked with a youthful step, however.

Reaching a door, she opened it. "Here it is," she said. "Let me know if it's what you need." With that, she was gone.

I closed the door behind me and looked around. What I need? An odd expression to use. Fundamentally true, though. I did need some place to hang my hat. (My cap.) I needed to give Miriam a much-needed breather from my presence.

There were two windows in the room. Through the one in front of me, I could see Church Avenue, the passing cars and occasional pedestrians. Nothing special there. I looked around the room. Nothing special there, either. The furniture was as elderly as I was, equally so. No private bathroom, of course. I'd have to share. Not a problem. The house was pleasantly quiet except for the motor hum of passing vehicles. The room would do.

I moved to the other window. It looked out on a barren lot. To the right was a view of Church Avenue. I looked at it for a few moments.

And felt my spine turn to cold water. I shuddered so violently that I visualized my spine collapsing like a thin tower and splashing out of my body.

It was Church Avenue all right. But not the avenue I was accustomed to. It was unquestionably—*incredibly*—different. In brief, I didn't recognize it. It was *different*. How different, I had no idea.

So what did I do? Old fool that I am, I raised the window and—bones creaking—climbed (clambered, actually) outside and dropped to the ground. The fall gave me spinal pain; now it was hard bone again. I ignored the pain and moved as quickly as I could to Church Avenue.

"*My God*," I remember muttering. (I muttered it innumerable times that afternoon.)

It *was* different. Totally different. Appearing as it had when I was young.

Young! I shuffled, unable to move distinctly, and looked at my reflection in the nearest store window. No difference there. My reflection was, as usual, that of an eighty-two-year-old man—white bearded (albeit well trimmed), face not too noticeably lined, white cap covering hair-receded skull. Not too bad looking. But still eighty-two. Church Avenue might have changed. I had not.

I looked into the store. It was a butcher shop. There was a sign printed on the window: ESPOSITO MEATS.

That cold, liquid sensation in my spine again. Johnny Esposito! The Y! The gang! Was that the time I'd reached? How old was I? Thirteen? Fourteen? What? "My God," I said again. (As I mentioned, one of many I muttered that afternoon.)

No, I was still eighty-two. But what year was I in? If Johnny Esposito was about, were Harry Pearce and Ken Naylor and all the others? Good God, could I walk up a few blocks, turn right and come to the YMCA? Would I see the old gang playing softball in the yard? *Hit the porch column and get a double!* Jesus, I hadn't thought of that in ages!

No. I had to shake my head. It was all too insane. What if I *could* reach the Y? What if I saw my young self playing in the yard? Pitching for the Ravens. Would I stare? Walk away? Yell to myself? "Hey, strike 'im out, Rich!" Impossible. Put the crazy notion aside. So Church

Avenue had changed. That was no reason to believe that the area for miles around had changed too. I was sure it hadn't.

Or *had* it?

Now the entire madness of what I was experiencing flooded through me. I had time traveled! I'd written television scripts about that, but now I was actually living it! Or was I dreaming it? Was I at home in Miriam's house, sacked out on my bed, fantasizing about my past? But, if that was true, why was I still eighty-two? Why was I experiencing every moment in my brain and body?

Only one way to validate. Keep moving. Keep looking. Should I try to find the Y? Probably not. I had no proof that this pocket of the past (insane notion) extended blocks beyond where I stood. Not knowing what had caused it in the first place, how could I be sure of its entirety? Better not, I decided. Stay on Church Avenue. Maybe that's all there was. Go the other way. The Y and what I might find there was really immaterial anyway. The gang was part of my youth but not so important a part that I had to see it. And God knew I'd rather avoid seeing my young self playing softball. More important things to see. And who knew how long this mad excursion into yesteryear would last? *I* didn't.

So I started—what, east?—down Church Avenue toward, I believed, Flatbush Avenue. The accuracy of my impulse was verified by the sight of the Kenmore Theatre marquee. I was able to see the letters. LITTLE MISS MARKER. The sight of it thrilled me. I'd seen it one afternoon after Sunday school. My sister treated my mother and me to the show; they were coming from church. How old was I? Twelve? Thirteen? Impossible to recollect, but I was getting close, I thought.

Before the show, we had lunch at Bickford's Cafeteria, which (thrilled again) I could now see across the way, on Flatbush Avenue; I was at its intersection with Church. *My God.* One remembered sight followed another. Now the Flatbush Theatre on Church Avenue just past Flatbush. I could barely make out the letters on its smaller marquee. BROOKLYN, USA. I remembered seeing it. The scene in the barbershop, the customer, (a gangster, I recalled) getting murdered with an ice pick. Scary stuff to a—what?—thirteen-year-old. Fourteen? And just down the avenue was the bar-restaurant where real gangsters met and ate and even married. I'd read about it in the newspaper when I was—whatever age I was, I still didn't know.

It suddenly occurred to me—at once thrilling and

frightening—that, if I walked further down Church Avenue, I might reach the ancient brick building I knew as P.S. 81. Was it still there? Why wouldn't it be? Unless this section of the past did not extend that far. That's the part that frightened me. Why was all this happening to me anyway? Should I stop someone and ask? No, that would be stupid. Everyone I passed obviously belonged in this time. I couldn't prove it, but I'm sure my expression was one of constant awe. No one I passed wore such an expression. They were in their time. I was the dazed interloper.

I wouldn't try to explore the size of the past world. If P.S. 81 was actually there, I was too unnerved to try reaching it. What if I did reach it? Would I see my young self in one of the classrooms taking instructions (in what? Grammar? Arithmetic? Geography?) from Mrs. Ottolengui? Good God, I remembered her name! That frightened me, too. Did it mean I was being absorbed back into this time? I looked at the backs of my hands in alarm. (Or was it with hope?)

No. Still old. As always, thickly veined in dark blue. I had not lost eighty-two years. *Jesus Christ, what's going on?!* I wondered in sudden alarmed anger. What was the point of it all? For a moment (but only a moment) I considered rushing back to the house and climbing back through that window. Except, of course (a terrifying except), what if the house wasn't there any longer? What if I was trapped in the past—a lone elderly gent caught in his own childhood?

No, that was impossible. There had to be *some* logic left in the world. Some sense to what I was going through. Why reverse time itself if there was no point to it? Why should nature distort itself so bizarrely for no reason?

All right, I decided (what other choice did I have?), I would continue and let the chronological chips fall where they may.

I crossed Church Avenue, wondering what the consequences would be of allowing myself to be struck down by one of the passing cars. A screech of brakes, an impact, the old gent flying to the pavement, most likely to his death. Who would gather up the body? Would my young self suffer the same fate when he reached eighty-two? Enigma piled on enigma. Would it happen again? A nightmarish possibility.

Anyway, I reached the curb safely, ignoring the angry shout of a motorist who had just missed sideswiping me.

In front of me was the Dutch Reform Church. I remembered playing basketball in its gym. A *gym* in a *church?* I thought, confused.

With that, the charm of it all returned. No point in dark conjectures about the mystery of an eighty-two-year-old man at bay in his own past. Enjoy yourself, I thought.

And so I did. Strolling down the Flatbush Avenue I recalled, newly moved by the sight of each spot I remembered vividly—at least when I saw it again. Loft's Candy. We used to buy a package the size of a pound of butter in which was a thin layer of frozen strawberries, a thicker layer of vanilla ice cream. Enough for three, my sister, mother, and me, or four if my older brother Bob showed up, *five* if his fiancée, Mary, accompanied him. God, I thought. Any of my kids—John, Arthur, Miriam—could have single-handedly devoured the entire package.

Across the way was the high school Barbra Streisand had attended. At first, I couldn't remember its name. Why not? I remembered Mrs. Ottolengui's name. Then it came to me. *Erasmus.* He was what? A mathematician? A philosopher? Greek probably. *So what?* I thought. Too many mixed-up, meaningless recollections. *Concentrate!* I ordered myself.

Which is when it occurred to me that Erasmus extended all the way to Bedford Avenue, a block away. How could that be? *Did* the past effect stretch that far? Had I merely been, for some unknown reason, a traveler back to an entire location? Was I in Brooklyn *completely*? If I took a BMT subway train downtown would it all be there? *For God's sake!* came the stunned notion. I might get so enmeshed in the past that I could never get back to that damned window. Then what? An eighty-two-year-old man from the year 2009 trapped in the year—what year *was* it?

I took a chance, risky or not. I stopped an old lady who looked kind. "Excuse me, ma'am," I said. "I'm lost. Could you tell me where I am?"

"Brooklyn, of course," she answered. "Flatbush."

"Ah," I said. "And it's nineteen hundred—?"

Her lips pursed. Now I'd irritated her. "*Forty-one*," she said as though addressing an aggravating child.

"Forty-one," I said.

"*Yes*," she said, "and, if you're lost, you'd better tell a policeman."

"Yes," I said. "Thank you so much."

She gave me a look which seemed to be one of suspicious curiosity. I didn't want to intrude on her any longer so I repeated my thanks and continued on down the sidewalk of 1941 Flatbush Avenue. I was pleased that I had (successfully, it appeared) invaded the past without repercussion. Of course, I had displeased that old lady—at the end of our brief exchange she'd grown cautious. *Why?* I wondered. Was my 2009 outfit so different? Or was it simply that my queries had been peculiar, even suspect?

I had to put that out of my brain. It was getting cluttered there. I stared at Erasmus as I walked, remembering, at that moment, that a few doors down from its Bedford Avenue side was the Jewish temple, (I recalled the sound of their chanting through their open back doorway) and, a few doors down from them, my aunt and uncle's house, next to that the two-story office building where they did cleaning and where they took me one evening with my cousin Frances to look at the mass of axed pinball machines, the result of a local police attack. And on the first floor was the ice-cream parlor where I bought Gob's ice cream cones—

Too much! My brain was being consumed by unnecessary memories again! I had to control them! I *had* to. I washed them off with deliberate focus. I was on Flatbush Avenue. I'd keep my self—and brain—exclusively

there, enjoy the nostalgic sights, not let my brain go hay-
wire with mobbing remembrances. *Good.* I would not
dream of ringing the doorbell of my aunt and uncle's
house. Assuming, as I now did, that the house was actually there, what impossible complications would arise
if they answered the door? A slough of incredible explanations consumed my brain. Yes, I know I'm eighty-two,
but I'm really fifteen; I'm your nephew Richard. I'm here
from the year 2009. I went out a window in a house
on Church Avenue and—lo and behold!—I'm in 1941.
Strange, isn't it?

Impossible, isn't it? I thought. Time traveling into one's
past had to impose certain rules, certain limitations.
One of which is: Don't try to think too much. Don't try
to contact anybody. *Just be an observer.*

All right, all right. I got it. So down Flatbush Avenue
I strolled, an observer in time. *Only.*

I went back to Loft's Candy and smiled at the display
of candy boxes in the window. Most of them were for
Easter. It must be April, then. A weekday in April judg-
ing from the movement of students in and out of Erasmus. The memory (I had to assume it was valid) that
Miriam's three boys were also in school. *Sixty-eight years
hence!* That thought startled me. I blotted it out and

continued my walk of memories. Before I left, I looked at my reflection in Loft's window. Still old, still white bearded.

Next, the pancake restaurant. A visual delight. I smiled as I watched the narrow stream of batter pour down on the revolving griddle. Watched the circles of batter—all perfect in size—bubble as they moved on the turning grill, then were flipped over as a spatula appeared magically to do so. And, at the end of this wondrous spectacle, another spatula, even more miraculously, placed three pancakes on each waiting plate. I watched this for about fifteen minutes, my face, I'm convinced, bathed with a constant smile.

Then it suddenly came to me that close by—nearly *too* close—was the stairway leading up to the second-floor dress suit rental shop and the third-floor apartment where I'd lived during much of my early high school years with my mother, sister, and brother. I say too close because it snatched back the adversity of time travel. If I went up those stairs and knocked on the door, would my mother open it? She might be working at Ebinger's Bakery, my sister at Abraham & Straus. What if *I* answered the door? Such an enigma was beyond calculation. He would stare at me, no doubt blankly. I would be speechless. Or, worse, babble some sort of stupid remark. "Sorry, son, I thought this was the tuxedo rental place." Utterly stupid. Could he possibly guess that I was an aged version of him? How could he? In any event, the moment would be embarrassingly awkward, or worse, frighteningly revealing. Most likely horrifying to both of us, especially me. No, forget that possibility. Just keep walking. God forbid I should ever confront my younger self during this incredible wandering. No, I'd just walk on.

Next block. Grant's five-and-ten. I crossed the street I used to walk to school on. Was P.S. 119 still there? I didn't mean *still*, I meant *now*. No point in trying to reach it. What for? The long walk to it—at least three quarters of a mile—would surely catapult me back to 2009. Then what? Try climbing out that window again? (Assuming it was even there.) Surely it wouldn't work a second time.

No, stay on Flatbush Avenue. Observe. Don't take any risks of losing this remarkable experience. God forbid trying to buy a souvenir. That would be a terrible mistake.

Grant's again. My aunt and cousin Vivian used to shop there the day after Thanksgiving. Or was it the day after Christmas? I couldn't remember which. Taking advantage of what they called rummage sales. Useless articles. At cut-rate prices.

On the next block down was Woolworth's, another five-and-dime store. And across the avenue was the small grocery store where, I recalled, during some kind of strike, buying a quart of milk for a nickel. And Pechter's rye bread for nine cents. And a pumpernickel for thirteen cents. *Stop that*, I told my crowding brain. *Just look. Don't dwell on memories of food.* Like a trio of cream-filled cupcakes for a dime. Like Dusky Dan stone-hard caramel lollipops for—

Stop! I ordered my losing-control brain. Just . . . *stop*.

But I couldn't. Past recollections kept infusing my consciousness. Merkel's Meat Market across the avenue. A pound of bacon ends for nineteen cents. How I loved the sandwiches my mother made from toasted wheat bread and fried bacon ends and mayonnaise. I devoured them for lunch in high school. If I ate one now, at eighty-two, the combination would nauseate me. But *then* . . .

And the fruit and vegetable store at the corner. I literally visualized my customary purchase, a nickel's worth of "soup greens," a full-size grocery bag loaded with carrots and onions and turnips and—

Jesus Christ, cut it out! I begged my brain. *Just look!* But I couldn't control it. On the next block, the Loew's Kings where I saw the Marx Brothers in *A Day at the Races.* Further down, the Rialto theatre where I saw *Gone With the Wind* in its later run. The Chinese restaurant, the bowling alley. Was there no end to this? Was that the peril of time travel? At least, the time travel I was immersed in. I had to stop; simply had to stop this endless discharge of pointless memories, this brainless gushing of trivia. But *how?* I stopped walking and pleaded with myself. *Do something right*, I begged.

Then it occurred to me.

Adeline.

Of course! How had I missed it? If there was any reasonable *point* to all this, it was Adeline, my first and only love. But where was she? Was it possible that she was, as I always remembered her, sitting on the porch of the Bedford Avenue apartment house?

Directly across the avenue from the third-floor apartment I lived in with my mother and sister? The third-floor apartment where I stood at the window of my mother's bedroom, looking across the way? Staring at Adeline.

Why had I never had the courage to cross the avenue and speak to her? Why, when I was totally in love with her? Remember, I was fifteen years old. There would be other females in my life. Jane on Long Island. Lucille in Brooklyn. Mary at college. Agnes in my life. But none compared to Adeline. My angel. I always thought of her that way.

Once, I stood right next to her in the delicatessen around the corner. Did I say hello? Say anything at all? I did not. I stood beside her in mute adoration, paralyzed by love.

I had to speak to her now. I *had* to!

Blindly—it was a marvel that I wasn't flattened on Flatbush Avenue, although I certainly evoked a number of outraged car horns and one clanging trolley car bell—I rushed up Albemarle Road. I had no idea whether Bedford Avenue was waiting for me. I never gave it a moment's consideration. I had to see Adeline. It was all that mattered to me. So I ran as fast as I could—which at eighty-two was of limited velocity. More a hasty shuffle. I didn't think of it, however. Didn't give a moment's thought to the possibility of a heart attack. I ignored my pacemaker pounding. Another stroke perhaps? No thought of that. Only one thing filled my mind. One word. One name.

I reached Bedford Avenue; it *was* there! I turned right and started up the block. My gaze leaped hungrily across the way. There! Two girls sitting on the porch steps of her apartment house!

One of them was Adeline.

I jarred to a halt, aware, for the first time since I'd begun running, that I was panting for breath. I stared across the avenue. It *was* her, wasn't it? Yes, it had to be. Her hair, that golden wreath around her head. It was unmistakable. To me anyway. The vision had been imprinted in my brain for sixty-seven years.

That brought me up short. I wasn't fifteen anymore. I was an old man.

No, that wasn't so! I looked up at the window of my mother's bedroom. I couldn't see from that angle. Without a thought, I crossed the avenue and looked up again.

There I was at the window, gazing intently at Adeline. I drew in a shaking, almost gasping breath. Can you imagine what it would be like to see your own younger self? Your actual younger self? And know what that younger self was thinking?

And yet I *didn't* know. I wasn't *there*—inside his head, his brain. I knew what he was thinking but I wasn't inside his brain. A minor discrepancy perhaps, but, to me, all important.

I had to act as what I was at this moment: eighty-two-year-old Richard Swanson. Determined to not only see the past up close, but to change it. I turned and walked closer to the porch where Adeline was sitting with her friend, the little Italian girl named—I couldn't remember her name, was it Luisa? I thought for a second that younger Richard might be watching me approach the porch. How could he miss it? Wouldn't he wonder who I was? Wouldn't it disturb him? Was I breaking one of the cardinal rules of time travel—making contact with the past? *No*, I told myself determinedly. It was a rule I'd come up with myself. No one had transmitted it to me. So to hell with it. To ruddy, bloody hell with it! I was *here*. With Adeline. *I could change everything.*

I stopped in front of the porch and gazed at her, my angel. She was still that. Memory had not deceived. She *was* beautiful. Incredibly beautiful. *I love you*, I thought. *I've always loved you.*

They had seen me stop; now saw me staring.

"What d'ya want, old man?" the Italian girl demanded.

That puts me in my place, I thought.

Then occurred the most horrible event in the entire experience.

The same tongue-tied inability to speak which had assailed me in the delicatessen that afternoon now took place again. I wanted—desperately—to tell her who I was. That my younger self was, at that very second, gazing at her through a window across the way. That he loved her now and that I, the old man standing in front of her, had loved her always. That, somehow, she must speak to my younger self. Get to know him. *Love him as he loves you. Now. This year.* And always.

I couldn't say a word. Was it me or was I prevented from speaking because I *had*, after all, broken that rule of time travel?

How long I stood there, a mute statue called *wordless love*, I had no idea. It must have been long enough to disturb her though. "Why are you staring at me?" she asked.

Because I love you, damn it! yelled my brain. But my tongue, my voice? Still paralyzed.

Then Adeline said one thing I will always remember, always cherish.

"Are you all right?" she asked. Concerned. Loving. I will never forget that.

Her words were disfigured in a moment by the Italian girl snapping, "Get outta here, old man! We'll call a cop!"

That did it. The moment was lost. Without a word—completely unavailable to me anyway—I turned and walked away. Cursing myself inwardly. *For Christ's sake, go back and tell her what she has to hear! If you don't, that poor, speechless sap in the window will never say boo. And all will be lost. As always, dammit! As bloody* always!

I don't remember how I got back to Flatbush Avenue. Not a step of it. I know I must have passed the police station, the Edison store. Not a glimmer of recollection. Only one thing remembered. Sitting on one of the steps to our old apartment.

And seeing myself walk by.

My immediate inclination was to shrink back in startled avoidance. Not that much of a problem since he had already passed me by.

How do I describe my feelings at that moment? There

was a fascination, no doubt of that. But also discomfort, even dismay. Why? Think of it. You—eighty-two—looking at your fifteen-year-old self walking by. Moments of distress at the duplicate reality. *Two of you*, one fifteen, one eighty-two. How could the confused sensation be allied? No way. I had to just accept the anomaly.

Then it struck me: I had a choice. There were no hard-and-fast rules controlling time travel. I was free to act as I chose. *I could alter anything at will.*

So I stood quickly and hurried after myself. Sounds crazy, doesn't it? It *is* crazy. The whole experience was crazy. With one exception.

It happened.

So there I was, my old self striding confidently (willfully at any rate) after my young self. "Richard!" I called, suddenly remembering that the gang at the Y called me "Swanee." Would he respond to that nickname more readily? Probably not.

He didn't turn, kept walking. I recognized his stride, smiling as I remembered how my mother described it as loose and wobbly. It was that.

I called his name again. This time he heard me and stopped to look around. I approached him—and let me tell you about the uncanny encounter of standing inches from your own younger self. The feeling goes beyond description. It was, at once, thrilling and frightening.

"What is it?" he asked. Not too politely. Who was this old guy and what did he want?

I tried to start what I meant to say, suffering an abrupt dread that I was about to face the same dumbstruck inability to speak that I had experienced in front of Adeline. I fought it off. I would not let it happen again! "I want," I began, then faltered. "I want to help you," I blurted.

"Is this some kind of charity?" my fifteen-year-old self asked suspiciously.

I felt a tremor of amusement. I'd always had a skeptical nature. I had to smile. My show of diversion didn't please him. He turned away. "No, don't," I said abruptly.

He turned back. "Listen, *sir*," he said. The *sir* did not sound at all polite.

"I want to speak to you about Adeline," I said.

He stared at me. "*Who?*" he asked. He sounded far more aggravated than curious.

Mentally, I jumped back in my own time. Had this ever happened to me when I was fifteen? I was sure it hadn't. This was something else. Something else entirely. I was transcending time travel.

Which strengthened my resolve to say, "The girl who lives across the street from you. The one you look at from the window of your mother's bedroom." There. I'd said it. Time was changed.

My fifteen-year-old-self was looking at me with deep suspicion written on his face. He didn't speak.

"You have to speak to her," I told him.

"What are you, a detective or something?" he replied. I, my dubious teenage self, replied.

"No," I said, amused again.

He didn't react well to that amusement either.

"Listen, mister," he began.

"No," I interrupted him. "*You* listen. Adeline—"

"*How do you know her name?*" he demanded. He was really suspicious of me now. Was it all going wrong?

I couldn't let it go wrong. So, mistakenly or not, I countered him. "You don't know her name, do you? You don't know anything about her."

"*Listen*, mister," he started again.

"No, *you* listen, son!" I broke in again. (Of course, he wasn't my son, he was *me*.) "You have to speak to her. Stop staring out the window and go to her when she's sitting on her porch. Get to know her. Tell her you love her. That you want to spend the rest of your life with her. Don't make the same mistake *I* did! You've got to—"

"*Mister!*" he cried, cutting me off. "I don't know what you're talking about! All I know is you've lived your life! Now let me live mine!"

He was right, of course. I knew it in an instant. I had no right to mess with his life. I knew that he would never speak to Adeline. Would live his life without her. My attempted intervention was a waste of time. Would he even remember it? Doubtful.

I watched him walk away from me, my young self leaving me behind. Living his own life. As he had a perfect right to do. Unhampered by me. I'd tried in vain. . . . Time travel? Bah! Humbug!

Unless . . .

Unless it taught me something. But what? Leave yesterday alone, maybe. No point in trying to change the past. It's *gone*. Only in memories. Which are, face it, indelible; not subject to rewriting.

I walked back to the house. It was still there. I rang the deafening bell and the old lady opened the front door.

Somehow, it was 2009 once more. I don't have to climb back through the window. "I've decided against renting that room," I told her. She didn't seem surprised. "Thought you might," she said, then shut the door.

I walked back to Miriam's house. She'd returned from the market and was unloading groceries.

"Where you been, Dad?" she asked.

I kissed her on the cheek. "Went for a walk," I told her.

TOR

Award-winning authors
Compelling stories

Please join us at the website
below for more information
about this author and other great
Tor selections, and to sign up for
our monthly newsletter!